QUARAN AND TRINITY II:

A Chicago Love Story

A Novel by *Shy*

VISIT

WWW.AUTHORMISSCANDICE.COM

TO JOIN OUR MAILING LIST!

For exclusive sneak peeks and notifications of upcoming releases!

PREVIOUSLY

"I just hit them niggas up, they know wassup." Dame said.

We were posted up at Scooter's crib. It was time for this fuck nigga to meet his maker. As you know I'm a laid back type of nigga but disrespect wasn't tolerated. I sat back way too long, letting niggas slide. I didn't want to go back to the old me, but niggas wanted to test me like I wasn't a God out here. Murder was a game that I mastered. I tried to keep this savage buried but there was always some pussy ass nigga that thought he could escape death. Why did niggas want to test me? I was trying to get on the straight and narrow and turn this money legit. Something always got in the way of that though. I'd been spending too much time and losing money with this nigga running around.

"Aight cool," I said tucking my pistol in my waistband.

The sun was setting and people were probably in the crib getting ready to go out. That rat Jade had given Chevy word that were all supposed to be out partying tonight. Ima catch that bum ass nigga soon as he stepped foot out the crib. Either this bitch Jade was dumb as fuck or she just ran her mouth too loosely. Gossiping ass rat; I couldn't stand those types of bitches. Bitch didn't have any type of street smarts. That was the main reason I didn't run around with just any bitch. People walk around with these hidden ass agendas and you never know who you dealing with. Jade for instance; running around telling all this nigga's business without a care in the world. She didn't know Chevy from a can of paint but she was willing to offer up info without any questions asked. Dumb bitch didn't even know she was helping this nigga to his last breath.

"They just pulled up," Dame said looking out the window.

Chevy and Los hopped out the black Suburban and mobbed up to the front door. These niggas were always ready for war. That's why they were closest to me. I know Dame was thirsty as fuck to be getting his hands dirty right now. He was always down to murk a nigga. Didn't matter the reason. These were the type of niggas a boss needed around him, loyal and down for whatever.

Once they walked in the crib, I gave my directions.

"Nobody buss a move until I say, understood." I asked looking at every one of them.

They nodded in agreeance.

"I'm deading this nigga soon as I put eyes on him." Dame said grabbing the street sweeper off the coffee table, "Nigga done cost us too much money."

"Bro, chill. You gone get your excitement."

Dame was too damn amped up with his trigger happy ass. I appreciated him for wanting to handle shit but I didn't need any sloppy shit happening. I wanted Geno and his niggas hit, no innocent kids or women. That sloppy extra shit was out the question.

Once I finished giving orders, we suited up and headed to the back to the Suburban once Los pulled it to the back. I sat in the front beside Los and the rest of them hopped in the back. We rode in silence; I assume everyone was mentally preparing themselves. I sat thinking as well. I haven't had to off me a nigga in over a year. I didn't like doing this type of shit but it came with the territory and what had to be done, will be done. I was far from a pussy nigga, but I would rather not have to murk niggas. Shit was smooth when niggas played their part.

I sat in the passenger seat listening to Future flow through the speakers.

Laying low in a Maybach

Spraying at you like an Arab

Streets having you going crazy

I got my young niggas going crazy

Masked up nigga everyday

Got the sharp stick with me everyday

Half a pound in the ash tray

Burn it down nigga while I wait

Burn it down on good drink

On good drink, on good drink

Money long get your money long

Get these yellow diamonds I ain't had to call

Ridin' low like an esse

Getting doped up that's everyday

Hermes on me every day

Keep some Cartier on me every day

It was almost game time; we pulled up on Morgan and parked a few houses down. Wasn't too much out the norm. There weren't any kids out, which was a plus for me. Los creeped down the block and turned the music down. There were a few niggas sitting on his front porch. I'm sure they had burners on 'em. I wasn't worried about that though, this vest tucked under my hoodie had me taken care of.

"What it look like boss," Scooter asked from the back.

"Wait a minute," I said scoping out the perimeter making sure wasn't any pussy ass CPD cars riding around. "I don't even see the nigga out here."

We were still a few houses down and the sloppy ass niggas on the porch wasn't paying us any attention. Now true enough, I could ride down on niggas now and air they asses out, but I needed Geno in the midst of this. I didn't need any bullets flying if they weren't aimed at his tough ass. His niggas could get it too, but if I played my cards right, I could end it all right here. I shoot and he not here, what good would that do me? I'd be sitting around waiting for another retaliation and I didn't have time for that fuck shit. I wanted to get back to my normal routine and that didn't involve, murdering thirsty ass niggas who thought shit was sweet.

"Aye bro, that front door just opened," Scooter said as Los began to pull up closer.

"There go that pussy ass nigga right there," Dame said lowering his window.

I spotted the nigga sitting on the porch, chopping it up with the young niggas on the porch. He was outside kicking it like shit was gravy. He didn't have a care in the world while he pulled from the blunt he was smoking, like he didn't know niggas was looking for him. He must not know who the fuck Q is. There's no way possible, he's this careless and he's been out here doing dirt. The nigga couldn't have heard the stories about me, there's no way he could have. Or else, this nigga pussy nigga would have been hiding out, trying to save his life. Then again, he must not know that word got out he was behind the hits. Either way, it was time for his people to lay his ass to rest.

We pulled up in front of the house and Dame and I slowly lowered our windows. As soon as I was about to give word, I saw her pretty face coming out the front door. Trinity? By then, niggas on the porch were alert and by *then it was too late. I heard the shots ringing out from behind me.*

"DAME! NO!" I yelled.

It was too late, I saw her body collapse and my heart sank to the pit of my stomach.

QUARAN

You ever felt like your heart had been ripped out your chest? Well that is how I was feeling right now as I stared at the sleeping beauty laying in this hospital bed with tubes and machines hooked up to her. Being in this room with her gave me an eerie feeling. It was like I was stuck in a padded room about to lose my fucking mind. How the fuck did this happen? This is not how shit was supposed to go. We were supposed to ride down on niggas and end this bullshit. Instead, my baby was sitting in this hospital bed with a gunshot wound to her shoulder, all because my trigger happy ass, right hand man couldn't control himself. Dame was probably somewhere in this hospital too. I beat him nearly to death. If it wasn't for Scooter and Chevy, he would be a dead man. For as long as I have known Damien, I never thought he would slip up like that. A simple ass mistake could have cost Trinity her life.

BEEP, BEEP, BEEP!

The machines she was hooked up to just kept beeping, stirring me from my thoughts. This was like another nightmare. I had already loss my ex. If I loss Trinity, I don't know what I might do. Shorty came into my life and put her mack down on a nigga. I laughed to myself at the thought. Seriously though, I had developed feelings for shorty that I never expected too. Never in my twenty-nine years did I think I would fall for someone so fast. I guess it's true what they say, love comes when you least expect it. Now look at me, about to murk off my man's for my lady. I was so pissed at him; I don't know if I could ever forgive him.

I had my face resting in my hands when I heard a soft knock on the door. I glanced up and saw Trinity's mother and father coming inside. I stood up to greet her mother with a hug and her pops with a handshake. Her mother's face held an expression of sadness. That furthermore fucked up my mood, this shit was killing me.

There was another knock at the door. A petite black woman, with a short curly fro walked in with a clip board in her hand. It was Trinity's doctor; Dr. Johnson. She gave us a slight smile before she began to speak. "Good morning everyone, I came bearing good news. Trinity doesn't look to have any severe nerve damage. So with a few months, maybe less of therapy she'll be as good as new."

"How long before she wakes up?" her mother asked.

"A few hours, she'll be in a minimal amount of pain. I see they've given her morphine for the pain and discomfort." Dr. Johnson said.

Baby girl had come out of surgery a few hours ago and she was still out. Her beautiful face looked so peaceful as she slept. I couldn't wait until she got the fuck up out of here. This hospital shit was depressing as hell. I promised myself that when she was able to move around, that she would be living with me. I needed to make sure she was safe at all times. I thought pushing her away was benefiting me and all it did was fuck her up in the process. If I would've been around like I should have been, she would have never went running back to that pussy ass nigga Geno. Speaking of him, his ass is still breathing which is a major problem for me; a problem that needed to be handled pronto. The nigga had it coming to him one way or another.

I sat quietly in the corner of her room, next to her bed rubbing her small hand. Her parents were still by the door talking to the doctor. After shaking their hands, Dr. Johnson excused herself, Terrance and his wife came over to Trinity's bedside.

"Q, you need to go home and get you some rest sweetie. You've been sitting up in this hospital for hours. Have you eaten anything?" Trinity's mother asked.

"Nah, I'm good Mrs. Hayes. I'll be here until she wakes up." I said, maneuvering in the chair to get comfortable.

She smiled at me, "Q, I won't let anything happen to her while you're gone. If she wakes up, you'll be the first person I call."

I sighed, thinking. A nigga was tired as hell. I definitely needed a shower and a change of clothes. This chair was uncomfortable as hell and my body was sore as a mothafucka. I stood up and stretched. Trinity owed me something serious when she was better. I couldn't wait until she was better. This whole situation was fucking up a few things I had planned.

I stood up, "Aight Mrs. Hayes, you win. But please don't hesitate to call me if anything happens."

She walked up to me and embraced me, "I won't. Get you some rest."

Terrance stood up and dapped me before telling me the same. Her parents were cool as hell and they liked a nigga. I had known Terrance previously through my pops, so he had always fucked with me. They watched as I sluggishly walked over to Trinity's bed and kissed her forehead.

I left out of the room and headed back down to the lobby. I thought about checking to see if Dame was here, but decided against it. Fuck him right now. That was still my brother, but the way I was feeling right now, I would probably put hands on him again. My mind was still puzzled as to how he could be so stupid. He had never been a careless nigga. He had always been hot headed, but never careless. Nigga must have really been eager to get his hands dirty this time. I guess some of the losses we took, had him heated. That shit could easily be replaced. Once his ass was better, we were definitely gone have to chop it up. Bro didn't even try to fight me back; he took that ass whooping like a straight up gangsta.

Once I made it to the parking lot, I searched around for my Audi. I fished the keys out of my pants, hit the lock, and climbed inside. Fuck sleep. I was about to head home, change my clothes, and get back to my Trinity. My mind was fixed on her and this fucked up situation I had her in. If I ain't know any better, I would swear I was in love. I was cool with that though, what better woman than her? In my eyes, lil mama was the coldest. Everything about her was perfect to me. I planned on giving her bad ass the world. It's my duty to make sure she's straight. So as long as I was breathing, she would have whatever. I owed her that much.

After she was well and out the hospital, her sperm donor was a dead man. I can't focus how I need to with her in the hospital. I was doing it alone this time. No army of niggas, no shoot outs, no innocent by-standers. Just me and his pussy ass. Man to fucking man. I didn't have time to be chasing this nigga around the city. So when I catch his ass, he got a couple bullets with his name on them. I've never been in no shit like this. My guess is that the nigga feeling some type of way over his baby mom's but that's his loss. I lucked up because he fucked up. Nigga should have been handling his business.

I pulled up to the crib and parked in my driveway. I got in the crib and hopped right in the shower. I needed to get back to the hospital as quickly as possible. I was already feeling like I had been gone too long. Crazy right? Lil mama had a hold on nigga. Speaking of, her mom's just text me and said she was up. I needed to get back to her asap.

My week had been eventful and right now I wanted nothing more than to be under my shorty. I needed my peace of mind back; I wasn't with this stressing shit. Shit was finally getting back on track with me. I was trying to legalize this money and set myself up for an even wealthier future. I wasn't trying to deal with this drug shit for the rest of my life. Once I was straight, niggas could have this life. I swear niggas don't wanna see a nigga on the up and up. Once this shit blows over, I'm moving Trinity and Gio away from this bullshit.

My phone began vibrating on my sink, interrupting my thought process. I spit the toothpaste down the drain and stared at the caller ID. Andrea. I swiped the green button to the right and answered.

"Fuck you want?"

She snickered, "Well hello to you too Quaran."

"Man shorty, wassup? I ain't heard from you in months."

"I know Q and I'm sorry. Damn, chill with the attitude. I've missed you."

Andrea was a chick I was messing around with before I met Trinity. We were somewhat serious until she upped and left town on me without any warning. Who the fuck does that? I saw myself possibly building with her until that bullshit happened. She was beautiful, had a degree, and was trying to become a nurse. She had her shit together and she was cool. After she left, I pushed all thoughts, memories, and feelings for her to the side. What else was I supposed to do when a chick claims she loves me and just ups and leaves? Forget about her ass, that's what.

Now here she is, calling a nigga like shits sweet. Nah, far from it. I didn't play these childish ass games with women. I was a straight forward, get to the point type of dude. I am a grown ass man, what I look like playing games? Andrea knew I didn't fuck around, so she knew what type of reaction she was going to get out of me. Shorty still probably sitting over there thinking I still had a soft spot for her. Andrea was full of herself like that. Swear the world revolved around her ass.

"Straight?"

"Yeah I have. Can we meet up somewhere?" she asked.

I rolled my eyes. Fuck is her problem? "Andrea, what could you possibly want after almost a year of not speaking?"

"It's important. I wouldn't have called you if it wasn't."

"Well ain't shit more important than what I got going on right now. I'll holla at you later Drea," I said about to hang up.

"Wait! We have a daughter."

JHALANI

"Hi, can I help you?"

I looked up into the eyes of a middle aged woman sitting at the front desk of the hospital. I was too busy texting to notice that I had almost run into the large oak desk. I smiled and gave her Trinity's name before she looked her up in the database. She smiled and handed me a visitor's pass. I thanked her and headed to the elevators. I was nervous as fuck to see my sis, sitting up in some hospital for a somewhat serious injury. Although they said she would be fine, just the thought that it could have been worse had me in a fucked up space. I always looked out for Trini and the one time I couldn't tag along with her, this shit happens.

Had I been with her and Sugar that day, I would have talked her out of going to see Geno. She could have delivered the news to him over the phone but Trinity thought serious conversations should be had in person. Some things were better left alone and Geno should have been one of them. There's something that I don't trust in Geno. I can't put my finger on it, but I felt like his sudden streak of niceness had motive behind it. Geno hadn't been father of the year in years. As soon as he sees Trini out in public with another man, he wants to play nice. I wasn't buying it.

I needed my best friend better and the fuck out of this place. I took in a deep breath as I stood in front of her room door. My Galaxy 7 started to vibrate in my hand. I glanced down and saw that a private caller was calling me again for the millionth time. I rolled my eyes and pressed ignore again. Whoever it was would have to listen to my voicemail again. I had been receiving these weird ass calls out of nowhere. This blocked ass number kept calling all day and night. Then when I did answer, it was quiet as hell. I wanted to change my number, but I've had it for years.

Shaking my head, I lightly tapped on the door. I heard someone say come in, so I pushed the door in. Tavia sat at the edge of Trini's bed just staring at her while Trinity talked her ears off.

They looked over at me and smiled.

"Hey sis," Trinity said, giving me a weak smile.

I leaned down and kissed her forehead, "Hey boo, how you feeling?" I walked around to the other side of the bed and hugged Tavia, "Hey lil sis."

Tavia smiled and hugged me back. She looked at Trinity and rolled her eyes, "Sis she needs to chill the fuck out. She been trying to get up and move around since I got here."

"Man, I'm just ready to get up out of here. I'm fine." Trinity said trying to move her left arm. Panic took over her as she realized she couldn't move it. "Call the nurse! Please!"

Tavia pressed the call button for the nurse while I stood at Trinity's side trying to calm her down. She had tears running down her face. She had me shook, I couldn't imagine what she was going through. I was hoping that this was temporary, so she could get back to her old self.

A slim, brown skinned girl walked inside the room with a warm smile on her face, "Hey Trinity, everything okay?" She asked standing at the foot of the bed.

"Why can't I move my arm!?" Trinity asked still in a panic.

"Don't panic, its normal with shoulder wounds. You have temporary paralysis in your left arm because a few nerves were hit. Luckily the bullet went in and came out. You're expected to make a full recovery though love."

Trinity nodded as a lone tear rolled down her cheek. The nurse reassured her she would be fine and went to get her a bag of morphine for the pain.

"This is some bullshit; I can't believe this." Trinity said lying back in the bed.

"Calm down sis. I'm about to leave and get Gio, so mama can come back up here." Tavia said. She kissed Trinity on her cheek and headed for the door. "See you Lani."

"Bye Tavia."

Trinity sat on the bed staring off into space. I could tell by the wrinkles in her brows that she was upset. I hope her paralysis doesn't last long so that she could get out of her funk. I hated that she was down like this. Shit, being immobile would fuck with anybody who's used to moving around.

"Sis, don't trip. You'll be out of here in no time," I said pulling up the chair next to her and sitting down.

She smacked her lips, "Not fast enough. You know who did this to me?" she asked cutting her eyes at me and then blankly staring at the TV plastered on the wall.

"Better not been Geno's ass. I haven't asked because I wasn't sure if you wanted to talk about what happened." I said. Shit, asking someone so soon about a traumatizing event was touchy. You never knew how a person would react, so I left it alone. Plus, I know Trinity and she would talk when she was ready.

"No it definitely wasn't his ass. So, I'm over Geno's crib, basically letting him know that I couldn't deal with our situation anymore. As I'm leaving out of the crib, Dame starts shooting at the porch full of niggas and I got hit." She said cutting her eyes at me again.

My mouth dropped. Shocked, would be an understatement. I didn't even know what to think. I mean, why the fuck would Damien even be over there? What fucking beef does he even have with Geno? And most importantly why would he shoot at my best friend? I couldn't believe it; or rather I didn't want to believe it. How could the man I wanted to be with do something like this? My feelings were crushed. This would explain why I haven't heard from him. His phone had been going straight to voicemail. Damn. This is fucked up.

"But he wasn't shooting at you, right?" I asked still in disbelief.

She turned her head to the side to look at me, "Nah, I'm sure I wasn't the target. But what difference does it make? I'm sitting in this bitch with a paralyzed arm because of it." she rolled her eyes and reclined back in her bed.

I get why she's upset but why take her frustrations out on me? I wasn't the one who pulled the trigger. I'd be lying if I said I wasn't concerned about him as well. We've been friends before the intimacy and I still care about him. I know Trinity and I also know how she thinks. She's going to want me to cut him off, but that wasn't happening. I was upset too, shit. The situation would be different if Dame intentionally shot her, but he didn't.

"Sis, I get why you're mad. But I'm sure his intentions weren't to hurt you." I said trying to diffuse the situation.

"Again, I know that," she said, "Don't get all worked up, I'm not saying anything to the police. I told them I don't know who did it. If I know you like I think I do, you just as worried about him. He's in this hospital somewhere too."

My ears perked up at that information, "Huh? Why?"

She looked at me and said, "Because Q beat the fuck out of him, that's why."

I sighed, "Well whatever. Look Trini, I don't wanna beef with you over this. You're still my sister and I love you. I'll deal with that other shit later. I'm just trying to make sure you straight."

"I love you too sis. I'm not trying to beef or be a bitch, it's just a lot for me right now."

"I get it." I said, "When are they saying you can go home?"

"My doctor said hopefully in a day or two. I'll have to do the therapy of course when I get discharged."

"Well, I'll go to therapy with you."

She smiled, "Thanks for dealing with me sis. I'm sorry."

"It's cool. I understand."

We sat and talked for another hour before I decided to leave and let her get some rest.

I made it down to the parking lot and checked my phone. I had a text from an unknown number. I huffed, swiping the notification to the right. What I saw sent chills down my spine. I literally felt the hairs on the back of my neck stand up.

Unknown ID (3:17PM): *I've missed you.*

It was Miles. My gut told me it was him. Fear instantly took over me. I struggled looking through my purse for my keys. For some reason I felt like I was being watched. I wouldn't be surprised if he was in the vicinity watching me. That thought alone had me fumbling with the locks to get inside my car. After climbing in, I checked my surroundings. Nothing looked out of the ordinary. But that didn't mean a damn thing. I took a deep breath, trying to calm my nerves. I stuck the key in the ignition and brought the engine to life. I sped out of the parking lot and into the direction of my parents' house.

Maybe I was tripping and someone was playing tricks on me. I haven't heard from Miles in over two months. But who am I kidding, who else would be fucking with me like this? I never took Miles for a psychopath but shit I never thought he would turn out to be a woman beater either. I shook my head as I thought about the way he used to treat me. You never really know what someone will do. I just want to know why he would want to start fucking with me after all this time. I thought he had forgotten about me. Well at least a part of me was hoping he had.

I pulled up to my parents' house and got out of the car. I hit the locks as I walked to the front door. My mother greeted me with a smile. She must've been watching me out of the window. Her and my father had become even more overprotective of me. Right now, I appreciated the hell out of her for meeting me at the door. My nerves were shot.

"Hey sweetie, what's wrong?" My mother asked following me to the kitchen.

I grabbed a Fiji water from the refrigerator and gulped it down. I rested my sweaty palms on the counter top and tried to calm my breathing. My mother stood on the other side of the counter staring at me.

"I think Miles texted me."

Her eyes grew big as saucers, "What?! How do you know it's him?"

"I don't. But who else could it be? I've been receiving these weird calls from a blocked number, then today, I got a text saying 'I've missed you'."

I cringed on the inside. I prayed like hell that someone was bullshitting with me. I can't deal with the thought of Miles stalking me, let alone dealing with it at all. Shits been cool besides this dumb ass beef with Strawberry and Jade. I'd been Miles free for a few months and it felt great. No arguing, no stress, no fighting, just living.

"Well maybe we should call the police just in case."

"No. I haven't received anything else since earlier. I'm okay," I said grabbing my bottle of water and heading up to my room.

**

I tossed my purse on my night stand and collapsed on top of my bed. My mind was doing numbers. The one thing I couldn't stop thinking about was Damien. I missed the fuck out of him. It had been a few days since we talked at all. What Trinity told me earlier was on my conscience heavy as hell. I just know that he didn't shoot her on purpose. I wasn't sure what beef Dame and Q had with Geno but whatever it was must have been serious to result in a shootout. I just wished Trinity wasn't involved. She's my best friend and I love her, but I know how this is going to turn out. She's going to hold a grudge like no other and I didn't need that.

Damien made me happy. He's made me happier than I've been in a long time. I shouldn't have to choose between him and her. But the way Trinity's attitude was set up, I would probably have to. Thing is, she's gonna expect me to cut him off, but because Q and him are boys, he won't have to. It's not fair. Am I wrong for wanting to be with a man that made me happy? True, Trinity could have died behind this, but shit it was her man that had the beef with him! I could tell by the way she was acting earlier that she's going to make this hard for me. But I guess I would deal with it when the time presented itself.

I grabbed my phone from beside me and tried calling Damien. On the third ring, I was getting ready to hang up when I heard his deep baritone come through the receiver.

"Wassup baby girl?"

"Dame!? Hey baby, where are you?"

He laughed slightly, "You miss a nigga huh? I'm chillin though, at the crib. Just got out the hospital a few days ago."

"Why?" I didn't want to make it obvious that I knew what was going on.

"Man some shit went down; I'd rather not talk over the phone."

"You feel like any company?" I asked biting my bottom lip.

"Yea, slide through."

After hanging up with Dame, I quickly gathered up my purse and headed back out. I sped the entire way to his crib. Within fifteen minutes I was pulling up in front of his house. I texted him and let him know I was out front.

I climbed out the front seat and nervously walked up to his doorstep. I anxiously waited, while rubbing my arms. It was still summer but the wind was blowing a cool breeze. The door swung open and Damien stared at me inquisitively. He was awaiting my reaction to his two black eyes and swollen jaw. To say the least, Q fucked him up pretty bad. He stood to the side and allowed me in.

It was dimly lit besides the lighting from the sixty-inch flat screen that illuminated his living room. I could immediately tell he was in a funk. He must have been in the same spot for a few days because there was a blanket, pillows, empty food containers and a few empty cans of pop scattered about. He walked over to the huge couch and plopped down and motioned for me to sit next to him.

When I sat down, I expected to smell a musky odor or funky breath but got neither. He must have been in a good enough mood to shower at least. He sat on the side of me staring at the side of my face.

"What?" I asked shyly.

"I know you see my face. Let's address the elephant in the room."

I sighed, rubbing his swollen jaw, "What happened babe?"

He ran down the whole story of how Q and Geno started beefing. He told me how the whole shooting occurred and that he wasn't intentionally trying to hurt Trinity. Which I already knew in the first place. She just happened to be at the wrong place at the most fucked up time.

"Bro ain't trying to hear shit. I understand though. I didn't even fight him back. Just let him take all his frustrations out on me. He pissed at me for this shit. I've never seen him this mad at me. I should've been more careful."

"True but you weren't trying to hurt her. Why can't they understand that? It was a mistake." I said running my fingers through his curly fro.

"Yeah, a mistake that could have cost shorty her life. That's why they're not understanding," he shook his head, "We're both lucky. Q would have murked my ass for real."

"I understand, I guess."

"I fucked up fa sho this time. I know bro ain't gone easily forgive me." He said running his hand over his face.

I could tell the situation was fucking with him heavy. Dame was usually care free and energetic. You could tell he was stressed out from the tired look in his swollen eyes. Even through his bruises, he was still fine as ever to me.

Usually, we'd all be out kicking it right now, enjoying each other's company. I couldn't take this sudden separation in our circle. Shit wasn't supposed to be like this. Ugh. I had to figure out a way to fix this. I just wasn't sure what it was going to take. I knew that I would definitely have to give it some time and thought. I wasn't about to let this ruin my happiness.

TRINITY

I had been in this hospital for about a week. I was beyond ready to go. My attitude had been shitty since I had woke up from surgery. I just wanted to get home to my baby and my own bed. I'd only seen Gio twice since I'd been here because I didn't want him in this germy ass hospital. I missed him so much though. I called my sister and parents all day just to talk to him.

If it wasn't for Dame, I wouldn't be sitting in here in the first place. I hated him for this. I understood that he was looking out for Q, but damn, learn how to fucking shoot. The nigga could have killed me. I'd forgive him one day, but as of now I don't see that happening. Not only was I shot, but my shit was temporarily paralyzed which meant no work for me for a while. How the fuck was I supposed to make my money? The thought of not being able to make my money pissed me off even more. I was very thankful to be alive, don't get me wrong. But all this other shit is annoying as fuck.

I shifted in the hard ass bed, trying to get as comfortable as possible. The thin ass gown I was wearing had me freezing. I promise as soon as I'm able to go home, I'm getting in my own bed and going comatose. I don't think I've ever missed my condo as much as I do now.

"What's wrong shorty?" He asked.

I looked up at Q who was sitting right next to my bed flipping through the channels of the flat screen in the corner. He'd been right by my side since I've been here. I appreciated the fuck out of him for it. He showed me how much he really cared about me. He literally had been waiting on me hand and foot. Made me love him even more than I did before.

"I'm ready to go the fuck home Q. I'm tired of being here. Sick of looking at these ugly ass walls, sick of wearing this fucking gown, and I'm tired of this hard ass bed."

"Chill shorty. You gotta do what you gotta do to make sure you straight. I need you out here, so suck it up." He said leaning back in the chair.

I cut my eyes at him. I understood all that but it wasn't changing the fact that I was ready to go home. I looked at Q while he looked comfortable as ever sitting in that small ass chair. I knew that was far from the truth but he was sucking it up just to be here with me. I was doing all this complaining while he sat over there and hadn't said a word about being cramped up in the corner of this room.

"You're right. I just want to kiss and hug my baby and get in my own bed."

"I'm right here baby, you can hug and kiss me all you want."

I smacked my lips, "Boy, not you," I said laughing, while he smirked at me.

"I know, I'm fucking with you shorty. But listen, you should be out of here soon. Just be cool."

"I'm trying. I wouldn't even be here if it wasn't for yo homeboy," I said rolling my eyes.

He sighed deeply, "I already know Trin. But that's already taken care of. What you want to me to do, kill the nigga?"

I looked up at him, "No. That's yo boy and I don't expect you to do anything other than what you've done. I'm still pissed at him and probably will be for a while. I just want y'all to understand that."

"Who is y'all?"

"You, him, and Jhalani. I haven't told anyone else who did it. Everybody else thinks it was random. I ain't trying to bring no heat his way. I understand it was an accident. But what if I wasn't able to sit here and talk to you right now?"

"Yeah but you are, so gone with that bullshit. Quit trippin baby. You here and you good. My man's paid his dues. Now let it go."

Tuh! If Q and Jhalani thought, I was about to let this go so easily. They had another thing coming. I mean, who their right mind would just let go of being shot by someone they know? Exactly. They could get the fuck on.

**

"Hello Trinity," Dr. Johnson said as she walked in with a manila folder in her hand.

"Hey," I said giving her a half smile.

"Perk up dear, I have some good news for you," she smiled showing her perfectly white teeth, "you're going home."

I instantly cheered up, "Seriously?"

She nodded.

"Thank God!" I said. Immediately I started to try to get up. But she stopped me.

She laughed, "Let me get your discharge papers and the instructions on how to take care of your wound. I'll be back shortly."

She left the room shortly after. Q looked over at me with a smile. He told me, he was happy I was going home. I knew he was tired of my shitty attitude, but he wasn't the one sitting in this hospital bed for a week. He helped me out of bed and helped me get dressed. He spun me around and looked at my backside.

I looked at him confusedly, "what?"

"You've been sitting on your ass too long, it deflated a lil' bit."

I hit him with my good arm while laughing, "Shut up, crazy."

He laughed and pulled me close to him and planted a kiss on my forehead and then my lips. I loved this man.

"You know I love you T, but your breath funky as hell." He said covering his nose.

My eyes grew big and I covered my mouth in embarrassment, "Oh my God!"

"I'm kidding baby, come here." He laughed pulling me close again.

I lightly mushed his head again and told him to get off me. He apologized and told me he was only joking.

Shortly after, Dr. Johnson brought my paperwork back. I was finally a free woman. After packing up my things, Q and I headed for the lobby. They tried to give me a wheelchair but I happily declined. I was tired of sitting for the time being. I wanted nothing more than to walk right the hell up out of here.

I called my parents and told them that I had been discharged. They were as thirsty as I was. My father said that he would throw some food on the grill just for me if I wanted to come over. As tired as I was, I took him up on the offer. Wasn't nothing like my daddy's bbq. Besides, the weather was beautiful and I didn't want to be sitting in the house sulking.

Q stopped me by place to shower and change clothes. I decided on a simple, powder blue Maxi dress and a pair of sandals from Aldo. This stupid sling I was wearing was going to fuck up any outfit I decided to wear, so I went with simple. Q helped me pull my sew-in into a ponytail. Even though he talked shit the entire time, I was grateful for his help. I added some lip gloss to my lips and we headed out.

I called Jhalani to invite her over, but she declined saying she was out with her mom. I called my boo Sugar next; I had missed her crazy ass. She had been checking up on me all week with frequent texts and calls. She was ecstatic to hear I was out of the hospital and happily took up my offer to see me and enjoy some good, free food.

When we pulled up in front of my parents' house, I spotted Gio and Tavia standing in the window. When I stepped out of the car, my baby's eyes lit up with excitement. The front door flew open and Gio ran up to me squeezing my legs tightly. I wanted to scoop him up in my arms and squeeze him back but this injury kept me from doing so.

"Mama, I missed you! You back home for good?" He asked holding my hand and staring up at me.

"Yeah baby, mommy's home for good."

"Yes!" He exclaimed. He turned to look at Q and said, "wassup Q?"

"Wassup lil man? Wassup Tavia," Q said nodding at Tavia who was still standing in the doorway.

"Hey y'all!" She said moving to the side to allow us entry into the house. "Girl yo mama and daddy so thirsty you home." She said leading us to the back patio.

**

"Girl, you a mufuckin gangsta now," Sugar exclaimed as we sat on the back patio, chowing down on some shrimp and chicken kabobs.

We were all sitting outside enjoying the weather. Q had invited Chevy over and they were talking shit with my father by the grill. My mom and sister, were sitting on the opposite side of the table from Sugar and me. We were having a good time talking shit and laughing. Gio was playing basketball with Sugar's two boys on small Fisher-price net my daddy bought him.

I laughed, "Sugar please. I ain't proud of this shit."

"I am sitting here," my mother intervened, giving us the side eye.

"Sorry ma," we said in unison.

"I'm just playing boo. I'm glad you good. I couldn't wait for you to get up out of that hospital."

"Thanks Sug, me either."

"What I tell you about calling me Sugar outside of work?" She said laughing.

"Why do you call her Sugar at work?" My ma asked staring back and forth between Sugar and I.

I stuttered, "Umm, well, because...uh she doesn't want any of the creeps at the casino to know her name."

"Hm..." My mother said, then excused herself.

Shit! Almost blew my own damn cover. Sugar burst into laughter as soon as my mama stepped foot in the house. Tavia seemed to think shit was funny too. She was doubled over in laughter, holding her stomach. I couldn't help but laugh myself. I didn't need moms to know shit about my occupation. I would tell her eventually. Just not now.

"Damn, that was close. Let me make a mental note to keep saying Candice. Bish, you almost got me bumped off." I said swatting at her.

She snickered, "Whatever. That was all you," she looked away then whispered, "Anyway, why Chevy keep staring at me?"

"Girl he look like he tryna take you down," Tavia said looking at Chevy who had his eyes fixed on Candice.

Chevy was a cutie. He had blemish-free brown skin. His eyes were a lil chinky and he had a nice set of full lips. He kept a low fade, accompanied with a goatee. He stayed in something designer with his icy ass jewels on display. He was cool as hell and low key, just like Q. I couldn't even stunt, Q had some fine ass friends. Even Scooter's fat ass was handsome.

"Shit, I don't mind that at all," she said smiling.

"Go shoot your shot then boo," I said laughing at Candice. She was one woman I knew who wasn't afraid to go after something she wanted. Especially a man.

I looked up as Q made his way over to me with a smile plastered on his face. Butterflies invaded my stomach as he approached me and wrapped his arms around me. He placed a kiss on my neck, as I melted into him.

"You good baby? You need anything?" He asked, standing back to his full height of six-foot three.

"Nah, I'm good," I said looking up at him.

Chevy came over and asked to speak to Candice privately. I laughed to myself; I knew it was only a matter of time. My friends were some bad ass women, he couldn't resist. Candice stood up and winked at me as they walked over to the other side of the deck. My nosey ass was all smiles as I watched them interact. Q poked me in my side to get my attention.

"Stop being nosey ma," he said as his phone began ringing in his hand. He glanced down and excused himself.

I sat at the table talking to Tavia. She was currently telling me about her new boo. Tavia was picky as hell when it came to men and who she let in her life. My baby sister was a no nonsense type of bitch. She wasn't the type of woman a nigga could walk all over. She demanded respect and I loved that about her. Mama instilled that in us from youngins. I slipped up with Geno's dumb ass. Never again though. I couldn't play myself like that again.

"Sis, I like him. He's been consistent and I fuck with that." Tavia said.

"That's wassup then. You know consistency is rare these days."

"True, but shit you found you a good one," she said referring to Q.

I smiled, "You right about that. Q in a league of his own."

"Shit, he got a brother?"

We shared a laugh. I glanced over at Q who was standing by himself. His face held a scowl and his brows were knitted together. He turned away from me and began talking into the receiver of his phone. I could tell he was pissed from his body language. Whoever was on the other end of that phone must have said something to get him riled up. I wanted to go over and ask what was wrong, but I decided to give him his privacy.

He blew out a breath and ended the call before shoving the phone in his back pocket. He went over and whispered something to Chevy who began laughing hysterically. Candice gave me a look and I shrugged my shoulders. I didn't know what the hell was going on either. Q walked back over to Tavia and I with a smile plastered on his face. You would have never known he was just going off on somebody. I wondered what the fuck that was about. When he wrapped his arm around me, I decided to ask.

"What were you just fussing about?"

"Nothing, everything is good shorty."

He was lying his ass off. For now, I'd let it go for the sake of the fun we were having. But something told me he wasn't being honest with me and I didn't like that. We said we'd always be up front with one another and so far I've been holding up my end of the deal. Q better get his shit together. I wouldn't hesitate to leave his ass if he started to get on bullshit.

QUARAN

"Get some rest shorty. I need to talk to you about some things when you better." I told Trinity while she climbed into her bed.

"What things?"

"I said we'll talk. Lay down."

We had just changed her bandages and she was fresh out the shower. Lil mama was ass naked, besides her sling, climbing into her bed. She was definitely happy to be home. As much as I wanted to tear into that pussy, I said fuck it and let her get her rest. Gio had stayed with her parents for another night to allow her to sleep comfortably. And she was more than ready to lay down and get some much needed rest. Being posted up in the hospital was uncomfortable as hell for me, so I can imagine what shorty was feeling like.

With lil mama home, I can focus on the task at hand. Getting rid of Geno and taking on this new task with Andrea. Her ass was bugging on some reminiscent shit and I wasn't feeling that. How the fuck shorty leaves, pop back up with a baby and expect me to jump for joy? Fuck out of here. She had been blowing up my phone like crazy and it was mad annoying. I had to deal with her quick, before Trinity found out. I hadn't mentioned it to her yet because I wasn't sure how to approach the situation. I ain't wanna scare shorty away because she made it clear she didn't want any drama. That was ironic as fuck seeing as though I've dealt with nothing but drama since I started fucking with her. I knew it wasn't her fault and I couldn't even count it against her.

After Trinity fell asleep, I went into the front room and sprawled across her couch. My thoughts were all over the place. I grabbed my phone off the table and called Scooter.

"Wassup boss?" He asked after the second ring.

"Any word on this nigga?"

"Nah man. Nigga went into hiding or some shit. Pussy boy spooked."

"Aight." I hung up and sat the phone beside me.

I sat on the couch contemplating on my next move. This nigga was going to make it hard for me to catch his ass. It was cool doe, I was good at the cat and mouse game. Nigga was getting caught and that was a must. I was cut from a different cloth than these new age niggas. If I hear a nigga looking for me, let's link up. Geno was running around acting like he was looking for me but was never around when I was. That was goofy nigga shit. A mothafucka ain't never gotta worry about Q running around town pump-faking. But I want this nigga touched, so he's getting touched, period.

My phone lit up and I looked at the screen. *This bitch.* "Fuck you want Andrea?"

"Why have you been being so mean to me Q? I just want you to meet our daughter."

"You being disrespectful shorty. I told you I got a girl and you steady blowing up my phone. How that look?" I said. I could feel my nostrils flaring, I was getting more and more pissed off.

"Q, I was your girl at one point. I know I fucked up, but at least give me a chance to explain why I left."

She was sitting on this phone acting like I gave a fuck about her sob story.

"Look, give me a few days. I'll let you know where to meet me. I got a lot going on right now."

She sighed, "Alright. That's fine."

I hung up and tossed the phone on the other side of the couch. I didn't feel like being bothered by anyone else. Since Trinity was sleeping peacefully, I decided to stretch out across this couch and get some rest myself. I pulled my cargo shorts off and pulled my v-neck over my head. I relaxed and closed my eyes, letting sleep take over me.

**

"Q, wake up."

I cracked my eyes open and saw Trinity standing in front of me. She was looking beautiful as ever. I could still see every curve on her body through her silk robe. She gave me a small smile and handed me a bowl of Captain Crunch. I smiled back at her and sat up.

"This is all my one-handed ass could fix without any help."

I laughed, "It's all good baby. Thank you."

She sat down next to me and rubbed the back of my neck with her free hand. Lil mama was still catering to a nigga, fucked up shoulder and all. Now you see why I fuck with her? She's proven to be nothing less than perfect. She kissed my cheek and stood up. She pranced off toward her bedroom to get her ringing phone I assumed. I finished up my cereal and went into the bedroom with her. She was sitting on the edge of the bed laughing.

"What you laughing at?"

She looked up at me, "Nothing, Candice crazy ass."

"Oh, well you straight baby? I need to go take care of some shit."

"Yeah I'm cool. Go ahead. Jhalani and Candice about to stop over here."

"Aight I'll call to check up on you in a lil bit. I'll be back later though," I said.

I threw my clothes on not even bothering to shower yet. I ran in the bathroom and washed my face and brushed my teeth. I grabbed my keys off the coffee table and headed out the front door. It was nice as fuck outside. Fall was slowly approaching but it was still nice out. I hopped in my whip and called my barber, Zo.

"What up my nigga," he answered after a few rings.

"Aye bro, I'm about to slide through. You got anybody in the chair?" I asked making a right and heading for the expressway.

"Nigga you know you good. Come through."

I hung up and sped up to merge on I-94. I was speeding through traffic fighting with myself on whether or not I wanted to meet up with Andrea. I needed to because if she did indeed have my shorty, I needed to handle that. No way in fuck would I have a kid out here and not take care of my duties. That would be selfish as fuck of me. I decided to shoot her a text and told her to meet me at the barber shop in an hour.

When I pulled up, it was packed as usual. I hopped out and walked through the parking lot. Niggas gave a few head nods and said what's up. A few of the hood rats that hung out up here were giving me googly eyes but I mobbed right past their asses. I would never entertain these types of bitches. I had everything I needed from a woman at the crib. Speaking of her, I couldn't wait to get my ass back to the crib to her.

I pulled the door open and walked inside, saying wassup to a few young niggas from around the hood. A few of these young niggas were trying to get put on but I wasn't having it. I threw these lil niggas some bread every now and then just to show them I cared. A lot of young niggas didn't have men out here to show 'em the ropes and give 'em advice. This drug shit was destined for me. Or else, I would have been playing in the NBA right now. If I could change the way things turned out for me, I would have. So if I could stop these young mothafuckas from being eager beavers and trying to jump into the dope game, I would.

Mace, one of my young homies, mobbed up to me with a sly grin on his face. He sat down next to me and held his hand out, "Aye big bro. I need to holla at you about something. Feel me?" he said dapping me up.

Mace was about twenty-one. When I met him, he was posted up at a gas station hustling dime bags. He was out hustling trying to feed his moms and baby sister. He was only fourteen and at a young age he'd become the man in his house. He was eager to learn and ready to work to make his money. I admired that about him. When he approached me, I couldn't put him on and have him out here like that. If he was looking out for his people, he needed to be alive to do so. I got him a job in one of my pop's properties doing janitorial work.

When we made it to Zo's office, Mace wasted no time speaking.

"Man big bro, word on the street is you got some beef with that nigga Geno."

I frowned, "Nah ain't no beef. The nigga out here on some hoe shit. Niggas act tough, but we both know how pussy niggas can be."

"Check it out though, I know where that nigga been hiding out at."

My ears perked up at the sound of that. This is why Mace was my lil nigga. He stayed looking out. My own niggas couldn't even figure out where this nigga been resting his head.

"Straight?"

"Yeah bro. He's been hiding out at his bitch mama crib on 35th." He said looking me in the eyes.

"Fuck is he hiding out for? Nigga got on bullshit with me. I'm just gone finish it." I said.

Mace tossed his hands up, "fuck if I know. But look, homie used to be in the streets tough. For whatever reason he fell off and now he mad you running shit. My homie say he even more pissed you banging his bad ass baby mama. I guess the nigga just in his feelings cause he ain't running shit no more."

I huffed, "man, niggas know they be on some pussy ass shit. It's good though, I appreciate the info young blood," I went in my pocket and handed him a hundo.

He pushed it back to me, "I'm good. You've looked out for me enough. I owed you this one."

"Good looking."

We dapped up and headed back to the front just as Zo's client was getting up. Perfect timing. Zo was a busy nigga but he always made time for a nigga whenever I called.

Thirty minutes later, Zo was finishing up. My phone was already ringing off the hook with texts and calls from Andrea. Her ass was bugging and I was about to let her know that. All this extra ass shit she was doing was unnecessary. I swear some females do the most for no fuckin reason. This broad was tripping on me for some shit she did. How the fuck does that work?

I stood up and tossed Zo a fifty.

After using the bathroom, I walked outside and called Andrea's annoying ass back. Thirsty ass picked up on the first ring.

"Hey, I'm waiting for you."

"I'm in the parking lot. What kind of car you in?" I asked.

"A silver BMW."

I looked around the parking lot and spotted her sitting a little further down the lot. I hung up the phone and walked over to her car just as she was getting out. Andrea was still fine as fuck. Her light colored skin was now bronzed from the summer sun. She stood at about five foot five and had a slim model-like build. Her honey blonde hair was cut short with those finger waves chicks be wearing these days. She curled her full lips into a smile as she walked up to me with her arms open. As much as I didn't want to hug her, I couldn't help it. She wrapped her arms around my neck and inhaled.

"Still smelling good as fuck these days," she said pulling back and staring at me with her round, chestnut colored eyes. She had her perky titties resting up against my chest.

I pulled away completely. Shorty thought she was slick.

"Thanks, but fuck all that. Wassup?"

"First, lose the attitude Q. I know you ain't really feeling me right now and that's fine, but you ain't gotta be so fucking mean." She said leaning against the hood of her car.

She was right. I didn't have to treat her like shit but I mean what the fuck does she expect? I know she don't think it's cool for her to be blowing me up like she has been for the last few days. I also know she don't think it's cool that she supposedly had my baby and didn't tell me.

"Aight. My fault ma. You right," I paused and took a deep breath, "but ain't no way in fuck you thought I was going to respond well to this shit."

She sighed, "I didn't, but I didn't expect to get treated like this either."

"Come on now Drea, then you blowing up my phone like you're crazy. I told you I got a woman. You think that shit cool?"

"Look Q, I'm sorry. I've been bugging, I admit that. You know this shit is out of my character. I've never been the type of bitch to do shit like this. But put yourself in my shoes. You know how I felt about you before I left-

I cut her off, "Cut that bullshit Andrea. If you felt some type of way about me, what the fuck made you leave? Who the fuck does that?"

"Q, I'm sorry. I didn't know how to tell you. You were doing so good for yourself. Everything was on the up and up. I didn't want to distract you, so I left."

I shook my head and stood there silently. I didn't even know what to say. Her intentions were good but what she didn't understand is that, a baby would have motivated me even more. Instead of her plan working in her favor, she made shit worse for me and she doesn't even know it. As much as I wanna believe she was trying to do me a favor, something told me it was more to the story.

"Andrea, is there any possibility that anybody else could be the father?" I asked blatantly.

Her eyes bucked, "Are you fucking kidding me? Quaran, you fucking trippin now. You know got damn well I wasn't sleeping with nobody but you."

"Baby, I don't know what the fuck you were doing in your spare time."

She pushed me and got into her car. I guess she was in her feelings but I didn't give a fuck. She brought the engine to life and rolled her window down. "Call me when you stop being an asshole." She rolled her window up and sped off.

Baby girl must have thought I gave a fuck about her being mad. I didn't. I had bigger shit to worry about other than her feelings. She'd be calling me again; I was sure of that. I would never not be there for my shorty if it's mine but we needed to get that settled first. Me and Andrea fucked around tough, but that didn't mean she wasn't doing dirt. I didn't put shit past her or anybody for that matter.

I walked back to my car and pulled my keys from my pocket. After I climbed in, I dialed Chevy up and put the phone on speaker. I rolled up a blunt while I waited for him to answer. Bad as I wanted to hit brodie up, I wasn't ready yet. Shit was still a little shaky between us and I think we needed the distance. I know you like damn, you chose a woman over ya mans? But nah, shits about the respect. I call the shots and if a mothafucka can't respect what I say, then maybe you need to be on time out. He thought his judgement was better than mine and that mistake alone could have caused us even more problems.

"What up nigga?" Chevy said, choking.

"Damn you straight killa?" I asked laughing a little.

"Yeah, this Kush smoke got a nigga choking. That new shit you got is straight."

"Good. Look I need you to ride with me right quick. Be there in ten."

I didn't even wait for a response. I pressed the red button and sat the phone back in my cup holder. I lit the blunt and sped out of the parking lot. I turned the radio up and let Lucci play through the speakers.

I woke up feelin' like a boss
Stepped in some mud wiped it off
Took a lost, then a took a lost, took some more now
I'm a boss
I woke up feelin' like a boss
I might just get a nigga knocked off
Might put some paper on ya boss
It cost to be a boss, I woke up feelin' like a boss

**

"Where we at?" Chevy asked sitting up in his seat.

I stared out the window at the numbers on the house a few houses down. The numbers matched the ones Mace gave me earlier. I sat quietly watching, not bothering to answer him. He was watching me, trying to see what I was on. I was in deep thought. I hoped like fuck dude appeared over here somewhere. I was ready to murk him off but not now. I wanted homie to think shit was sweet. Let the commotion die down some. Then, when buddy got comfortable again, I'd snatch the life right up out of him.

"Aye bro, there go that loose bitch Jade right there," Chevy said nodding his head toward the crib.

"That's Geno mother in law crib. She must be visiting her home girl. Call that bitch real quick, ask her what she doing."

Chevy grabbed his phone and put it on speaker. She looked down and smiled before picking up. "Hey baby," she said twirling her hair around her fingers.

"Wassup shorty, what you doing?" he asked leaning back in the seat as if shorty could see him.

She huffed, "Nothing, sitting on Strawberry porch. I'm waiting on my cousin to come pick me up. Me and Strawberry just got into it."

"Straight? What y'all get into it for? Aint y'all besties," he asked snickering.

She replied, "Man, I don't know about her sometimes. It's always some drama with these mothafuckas. I'm tired of her always talking about Trinity. She ain't even got no real beef with the bitch. Just hating on her. Ever since Geno got her sister pregnant, that's all these mothafuckas talk about. I'm tired of it."

My ears were zoomed in on their conversation. Shorty sat on that porch, talking cash shit like she wasn't still in the presence of their crib. She seemed like the type that wasn't into all the shit they were trying to involve her in.

"Why don't you stop fucking with the hating ass bitch then," Chevy asked, egging her on.

She sighed, "I need to. I ain't with all this drama. Shit, me and Trinity used to be cool," her voice got lower, "Geno even got these bitches over here cooking up a scheme to kill Trinity."

JHALANI

"You did good sis, I'm proud of you," I said climbing into the front seat of my car.

"Thanks boo. I'm trying. I need out of this sling."

Trinity and I were leaving her first therapy appointment. I promised her I would be there for her so here I was. She was in good spirits although I know it was fucking with her. My sis was used to being mobile and being able to move around freely. I was happy she wasn't allowing it to damper her mood completely. She and I had been on great terms lately. I tried as much I could not to allow Damien to come up in our conversations. He was doing much better and was focusing on trying to open up some new businesses, to occupy his time. He didn't want to sit around moping about Q not fucking with him.

I hoped like hell this shit blew over soon. Things were awkward now. I was used to it being the four us. We used to have so much fun together. Now we were all kind of separated and I wasn't feeling it. I never wanted to be in a relationship and not have my bff and boyfriend get along. Although he was the one who sent the bullet at Trinity, I prayed that we could all get over this and move forward. I needed shit back the way it used to be. I needed them more than they knew right now.

The creepy calls and texts had become more frequent now. I was sure it was Miles stalking me. The thought of him watching me and not knowing where he was, was fucking with my mental terribly. Every move I make, I have to make with caution. I felt like I was a prisoner in my own world. I was too afraid to be alone which is why I hadn't moved out of my parent's house yet. My mother didn't want me to leave anyway. If I wasn't home, I was either at Dame's or Trinity's. I was trying my best to never be alone. I'd even gone as far as to get my FOID card. Damien has been taking me to the gun range to practice shooting. As scared as I was, I wouldn't hesitate to defend myself if need be.

"Are you hungry?" I asked Trinity as we pulled out of the parking lot from the rehabilitation center.

"Very. Sug-, Candice wants to meet for lunch. She said her cousin is in town and she wants to get out," Trinity said reading a text from her phone.

"Shit, let's go. I'm starving. Where's she trying to go?" I asked turning on the radio and plugging up my aux cord.

Trinity looked down at her phone, "She said Grand Luxe."

My stomach growled a little, "Ooh, good! I could definitely go for some buffalo blasts," I said dancing to Drake as we sped to the e-way.

Grips on your waist
Front way, back way
You know that I don't play
Streets not safe
But I never run away
Even when I'm away
Oti, oti, there's never much love when we go, oti

I pray to make it back in one piece
I pray, I pray

"That's why I need one dance, got a Hennessey in my hand," Trinity blurted out causing me to laugh, "Sis, I cannot wait to get this sling off. We gonna have the biggest celebration."

"I already know boo."

**

"Girl where is Candice at? I'm ready to eat," I said flipping through the menu as if I didn't have my meal mapped out already.

"She said she's coming up now." Trinity said flipping through her phone. She then raised her hand, causing me to turn around.

Candice was walking our way with a pretty ass girl following behind her. She was slim, with short hair, and beautiful eyes. They made their way through the crowd and sat across from Trinity and me. Candice pulled her Ray Ban shades off and sat them on the table.

"Hey boos. This is my cousin Andrea. Drea this is Jhalani and Trinity." She said pointing to us.

"Hey," we said unison.

Andrea smiled and said, "Nice to meet y'all. Sorry we were a little late. I had to drop my baby off at my mom's."

"It's cool. We understand," I said.

"Aww, you have a baby? How old?" Trinity asked.

Andrea smiled again, "she's six months."

Our waitress walked back up to take our orders. We ordered a few drinks, while we chatted and waited for our food. Candice's cousin Andrea was cool. She fit right in and we all talked like we'd known each other for years. She opened up to us about her baby's father and how he was absent in her child's life. She was a bit heartbroken and wanted them to be a family but he had moved on with another woman. Her and Trinity were vibing because they'd been through the same thing. Trinity was very comforting to her because she felt her pain.

"Ok, enough of the tears. Let's enjoy this day please. Cuz, you'll be fine. Amaya will be just fine. She ain't wanting for nothing." Candice intervened, "I know how you feel. When Jojo died, I didn't know how I would take care of Jayden and Josiah by myself. But we're fine. Just stay prayed up boo."

Andrea nodded and dabbed at her eyes, careful not to ruin her makeup. I was glad Candice intervened because the sadness was ruining my mood. I was trying to enjoy this nice ass day. Summer was almost over and I was trying to enjoy every minute of it that I was able to.

"Now, can we move on to something a little happier please? I want to tell you bitches about my date with Chevy." Candice said with a smirk as she sipped from her Lemon Drop Martini.

"What!" Trinity and I said in unison again.

We all shared a laugh.

"Do y'all always do that?" Andrea asked laughing.

"Yup," we said again, causing another roar of laughter between us.

"Ok bitches, stop making us laugh. Be serious, so I can tell y'all about the date." Candice said still laughing, "But anyway. We exchanged numbers at your parent's crib T. We texted and talked for a few days, then we finally went out. He's so damn sexy and he has this arrogance about him that I love. But bitch, I'd be damned if the nigga phone wasn't going crazy." Candice said rolling her eyes, "y'all would never guess whose name was flashing on his screen."

"Who?" I asked.

"Jade," she paused, "now I'm not sure if it was her, but I'm pretty sure it is. It's just real ironic, ya know?"

"True, but make sure it's that bitch first. You don't wanna cut him off for no reason. Especially if you feeling him like that." Trinity added.

"Man I just got a feeling it's her though. With all the shit that's going on, especially with them bitches, it's just crazy."

"I'll ask Q about them later. He might know what's up." Trinity said, sipping from her water.

"Q?" Andrea asked as she stopped chewing her food, "Q as in Quaran?"

We all shared a confused expression. Trinity more than anyone. If I knew my sis like I thought I did, she was over there with her thoughts going crazy. Probably wondering how this chick knew Q. Apparently she knew him well too, calling him by his government. Trinity put her water down and was all ears, just as Candice and I were.

"Yeah, Quaran. You know him?" Trinity asked.

"That's my daughter's father." Andrea answered.

My mouth dropped. Did this bitch just say what I think she just said? She had to, because Candice was staring at her confusedly. Apparently, she didn't know that information either. But Trinity, she sat there staring at Andrea, unmoved. I didn't know what she was thinking. I was praying like fuck Trinity kept cool though. With all the shit she was currently going though, I know that's the last thing she wanted to hear. Trinity nodded and excused herself. She headed for the bathroom. I started to follow her but she stopped me. She wanted to be alone to process the information and I understood.

I sat down and Andrea was looking back and forth between Candice and I.

"Did I say something wrong?" Andrea asked.

"That's her boyfriend." Candice answered.

Andrea huffed, "So she's the bitch Q been playing me for..."

I intervened, "Bitch? Watch your mouth about my best friend ho."

This ho had a lot of nerve trying to come for Trinity. Not only did she drop a shit load of tea on us but the bitch had nerve to be trying to stir the pot. Trinity ain't did shit to this bitch. How you mad 'cause a nigga played you for another woman? I don't know the full story about her and Q but I know for a fact he ain't the type of nigga to ditch his kid. This bitch Andrea wasn't telling us the full story.

"Drea chill. These are still my friends and you not about to disrespect them." Candice said turning to face Andrea.

"Really cuz, you choosing these bitches over me?" Andrea spat angrily.

"Candice, tell your cousin we ain't gone be too many more bitches." I said sitting my food back on the plate.

"I got her Jhalani," Candice said, "Drea, how you mad at her about Q not being there for your baby. Obviously she didn't even know the nigga had a baby and you wanna jump stupid with her," Candice said gawking at Andrea.

Andrea was visibly pissed. Her brows were knitted together and she had her bottom lip pulled into her mouth. Her knee was bouncing up and down while she sat quietly staring ahead. I was really sitting here trying to figure out what her deal was. This ho was really mad. It took everything in me to keep quiet and not go off on her. The silence at the table was awkward as hell and the tension was thick. Everybody was consumed with their own thoughts.

I shifted nervously in my seat as I spotted Trinity coming back to the table. I didn't know what to expect as she took her seat with a cold expression on her face. My best friend was pissed. She grabbed her glass of water and sipped, then looked at Andrea.

"So, you and Q have a baby together?" Trinity asked breaking the awkward silence at the table.

Andrea nodded, "I thought I just made that clear."

Trinity chuckled, "I'm sorry, did I miss something? What's your beef with me?"

Andrea sighed and looked up to the ceiling. This was a weird ass broad. For the life of me, I couldn't understand what this bitch's problem was. She was really sitting at this table fuming as if we had done something to her. If we were someplace else, I probably would have went off on her.

"Look, ain't really no beef. I'm just annoyed as fuck by your presence. If it wasn't for you, Q would be with me and we could raise our daughter as a family. He's got his head so far up your ass, that he's been being an asshole ever since I came back." Andrea said with venom dripping from her words.

Trinity held a smile on her face. She cleared her throat then said, "Baby girl, I'm not the reason that man ain't taking care of your baby. You are. Q ain't even the type of man to not take care of his seed. You sure you telling us the whole story boo?"

"What you mean? Of course I'm telling the whole story. The fuck I gotta lie for?" Andrea asked looking at Trinity.

I intervened, "Trini let's go. Stop going back and forth with her. She needs to take her attitude up with Q. Candice we love you boo, but let's end this here before it escalates. Call us later." I said going in my purse and grabbing a few bills.

As I handed them to Candice, she pushed them back to me, "I got it. I'll call y'all later."

Trinity and I exited the restaurant and waited for valet to bring my car around. This was not how this day was supposed to go. We were supposed to come here and chill, enjoy each other's company. Damn I wish Candice would have left her crazy ass cousin at home. I was terribly trying to rid myself of these negative thoughts. My phone vibrated in my hand and I looked down to see a text from Candice.

Candice (3:47PM): *So sorry about my cousin. I don't know wtf her deal is.*

"You get a text from Candice?" Trinity asked.

"Yeah. What the fuck was all that about?" I asked after texting Candice and tossing my phone in my oversized Gucci bag.

Trinity shrugged, "I have no idea. But best believe when I get to the crib, I'll find out."

"That shit just threw me all off guard. Are you ok?" I asked as the valet driver pulled in front of us. I paid him and we hopped in the car.

"I guess. I don't even really know what to think or how to feel. If he does have a baby by this bitch, that's gonna be a problem. Obviously the bitch is a little off. But I think I'm more pissed about the nigga not telling me. Like why the fuck I gotta find out from this ho?"

I understood. One thing I could agree with is that he should have told her. Nothing's worse than somebody knowing something about your boyfriend or girlfriend that you don't know; then having to look stupid when it's blurted out in front of you. That shit is all types of embarrassing. I don't know what I would have done if I was in Trinity's shoes. One thing was for sure though, Andrea was lucky Trinity is injured, or else, she would have had a well whooped ass.

**

My bath was everything. I was finally at home, relaxing in my bed. My body was tired and I wanted nothing more than to sleep. Today's events had me drained. I wanted to call Dame so bad and tell him about my day. Being that it involved some of Q's personal business, I decided not to. I didn't want to be messy. I needed to see him though, feel his body against mine. I'd sleep good for sure. Instead, I was home alone, bored and tired.

I rested against my headboard, scrolling through my Snapchat. Everybody was out partying and enjoying themselves, or booed up. Meanwhile, I was looking at them having fun. I exited Snapchat and laid down, getting ready to text Damien, but a text came through instead.

Unknown ID (9:34PM): *I know you hate being alone.*

A cool chill ran down my spine. I was paralyzed with fear again. I looked up at the clock on my wall. I heard a noise downstairs and I instantly reached in my night stand and grabbed my gun. I eased my bedroom door open and crept down the stairs. I swallowed hard staring at the shadowy figure by the front door. Whoever it was would have to die if that door opened. I took a deep breath and wiped my sweaty palms on my shirt. I raised my gun and aimed it at the door. The knob twisted and the door flung open.

"Jhalani! What the hell you doing?"

My heart was beating out of my chest. My chest heaved up and down as I stared at my father. He dropped the bags in his hands and grabbed me and pulled me into a hug. I broke down into tears as he held on to me. I needed to confront Miles. I couldn't live like this.

TRINITY

Pissed. One word to describe how I was currently feeling. I'm not even mad that Q could possibly have a baby with this chick. I'm mad that he didn't even tell me. Finding that shit out the way I did, was embarrassing as hell. One thing a woman hated the most was being embarrassed. I mean damn, didn't I deserve to know what was going on in Q's life? Whatever the reason Q kept it from me, better had been good.

I was currently sitting on my couch, sipping a glass of wine, waiting for Quaran to come through the door. As bad as I wanted to call and curse him out earlier, I quickly pushed the thought to the back of my mind. I didn't want any beef between us unless absolutely necessary. The old me would have went off and started an argument but I was trying to be better. Starting a fight would only make shit worse between us and I didn't need or want that right now.

I heard my spare keys jingling in the doorknob. I gulped down the last of my wine and sat the glass on the table. I wiped the mug off of my face because I didn't want to startle him. I just wanted us to have an adult conversation and figure out how to go from here.

He walked in and smiled at me with his hand behind his back. After locking the doors, he pulled his hand from behind his back and handed me a dozen pink and white roses. Butterflies instantly invaded my stomach. My lips curled into a smile as I stood up to accept my flowers. My arm wrapped around his neck and he placed a soft kiss on my neck.

"Thank you so much baby. I love them," I said bringing the pretty flowers to my face and inhaling their scent.

"I just wanted to get you a lil something. Let you know I was thinking about you while I was out." He said kicking his Jordan's off and sitting in my spot on the couch.

After placing the flowers in water, I walked back over to Q. He was stretched out, scrolling through his messages on his phone. Reluctantly, I sat down next to him and placed my feet in his lap. I was nervously thinking of ways to bring up the conversation. I didn't just want to blatantly ask him if he had a baby.

"How was therapy?" He asked. He grabbed ahold of my feet and began massaging them.

"It went ok. Hopefully," I paused, "no, I will be straight in a few more weeks. Mark my words."

He took his thumb and forcefully pressed it up and down the bottom of my foot, "That's wassup baby. I'm proud of you. I'm going next time."

"I had an interesting day though. Wanna hear about it?"

He nodded as he continued to make love to feet with his hands. The shit felt amazing.

"So after Jhalani and I left therapy, Candice invited us to lunch with her and her cousin from out of town. So we get there and she introduces us to her cousin, a girl named Andrea. Everything was everything up until I mentioned you to them and she informs us that you two have a baby together."

Q shook his head and said, "Of all the people Candice could be related to, it's that nutty ass broad. Look shorty, Andrea and I had something in the past. We fucked around tough until she got pregnant and left town shortly after. She didn't mention anything to me about being pregnant or having a fucking baby until a few weeks ago when she popped back up."

"Well, she around here running her mouth like you just a deadbeat ass nigga. She sat at that table and acted like you was the bad guy. Then the bitch had nerve to try and get snappy with me because you don't fuck with her anymore. Why didn't you tell me Quaran?"

He took a deep breath, "shorty, you don't know how bad I wanted to. When I told you I wanted to talk to you about a few things, that was one of 'em. This bitch has been blowing up my phone like crazy. Out of nowhere she calls my phone, talking about she wanna talk, and then she hit me with that shit."

I rolled my eyes, "she's gorgeous, but the bitch got a few screws loose. I can see why you liked her, but she's crazy as hell. Why don't you get a DNA test and be done with the bitch?"

"I planned to. Before I did any of that, I needed to make sure you were straight." He replied.

A smile crept upon my face, "I appreciate that Q, but take care of your business too. I'll be fine. This broad seems like a troublemaker and the only way to get rid of her is to get that DNA test."

He leaned over and pulled me into his lap, "So what if the baby is mine?"

"Do you really think I'd leave you or trip because you had a baby before you met me?" I asked.

He shrugged, "you know you women are crazy. I didn't know how you'd react."

"Well I ain't that woman. As long as you keep that broad in check, then we're good. I was just pissed about you not telling me. I didn't like being blindsided like that."

He kissed the back of my neck, "I'm sorry baby, I got you."

We sat on the couch and talked for hours. We were really getting to know each other. The last few months have been a roller coaster but I wouldn't have it any other way. I've been legitimately happy with Q. He's been everything I've ever dreamt about. I can honestly say that I think I'm in love. I never thought I'd reach this point again. Especially not after dealing with Geno's weak ass.

Speaking of him, I hadn't heard from him since that day I got shot. The bastard didn't even call to check on me or nothing.

The day I was leaving his crib, he was livid. I went over to talk to him because I wanted him to take me seriously. I could tell Geno a million times over the phone I didn't want to be with him and he'd still act like he didn't care. I went to deliver the news and to see how he was living before I considered letting Gio visit. When I got there and saw the numerous niggas hanging out and hood rats running around, I snapped. In the midst of the argument, I let him know that me and him didn't have a chance in hell to work shit out. He was pissed about me not wanting to be with him and working out our issues. Not only that, he was even more pissed because he knew it was Q that I wanted.

For some reason, Geno couldn't stand Q. He rapped about how Q wasn't shit but a street nigga, how he had different bitches out here claiming him, and how he wasn't good for me. I let that shit go in one ear and out the other. I wouldn't dare listen to Geno's no good ass rap about how another man wasn't good for me. Plus, Quaran hadn't showed me one ounce of disloyalty. So all that shit Geno was spitting at me, sounded like straight up envy. It was no secret that Q had taken the streets over and was running shit with an iron fist. People respected him as a man and a hustler. He made shit happen not only for him and his people, but he looked out for people in the hood. Geno was a selfish bastard that only looked out for himself.

I looked down and Q was staring up at me. He stared into my eyes with question. He had something on his mind and he was trying to figure out how to say it.

"What's wrong Q?"

He rubbed his beard and looked and stared at me, "What you think about moving into my crib?"

I sat there and thought about it for a minute. Was I ready for this? I've only dreamt about meeting a good dude and moving in together and having this perfect life together. Now here it is staring me in the face and I wasn't sure if I was ready. Things were happening so fast between me and Q that I couldn't fully wrap my head around it.

"You ain't gotta give me an answer now shorty. Let it marinate on you for a lil bit and get back to me."

"Ok. Just give me a few days."

"It's no rush. I'd just feel better knowing you safe and that I get to come home to you every night, permanently."

I blushed and kissed his lips. He was so fucking sweet.

"But check it out, my father gets out tomorrow and mom's having a lil' barbecue to celebrate him coming home. I need you there shorty. You and Gio. I've talked my pop's ears off about you."

"You know I wouldn't miss it. What time should I be ready?"

"Around three."

**

"Gio, where are your shoes?"

I was frantically running around trying to get us ready to meet Quaran's parents. Gio had been on his Xbox all morning instead of getting dressed like I had asked him too. Now it was time to go and Gio couldn't find his shoes. I had just bought these damn shoes not even a few days ago and they were lost already.

I huffed, "Gio baby, where did you last have the shoes?"

"Ma, if I knew that I wouldn't be looking for 'em," he said showing his missing two front teeth.

I laughed. I swear this little boy was getting too grown for me, "Boy go look in the closet in the living room."

The pressure to look nice was on today. I had to make a good impression on Q's parents. Trying to decide on the perfect look was stressful as hell. I didn't want to overdo it. I decided to not wear any makeup today. My mink lashes and lip gloss would just have to do. I stared at my reflection in the mirror, admiring my curves in my all black floor length maxi.

"You look pretty mommy, I found my shoes," Gio said holding the latest pair of Jordan's in the air.

I smiled, "thanks baby. Now go put your shoes on so we can go. Q should be pulling up in a minute."

I stared at my arm in the sling and shook the thoughts of depression that tried to creep up on me. Fuck that down and out shit today. I just needed to be myself. Q said his mama didn't play about him and she shouldn't.

She raised a good man. I didn't want to meet her while I was in a funk, so I quickly shook any negative thoughts. I slipped my pink painted toes in my metallic gold and black Michael Kors slides. I went to my room and fingered through my loose curls courtesy of Jhalani.

She came through earlier and said that her and Dame were coming too. I wasn't sure how I felt about seeing him, but I knew it would happen sooner or later. I promised myself I wouldn't trip. Today was going to be a good day.

A text alert popped up on my phone from Q.

Q (2:45PM): *Outside.*

I quickly replied and grabbed my metallic gold MK purse and told Gio to grab a jacket for later. I threw my purse over my neck and locked up the house while Gio ran downstairs to Q's Audi truck. When I got outside Q was strapping Gio in his seatbelt. When he closed the door, he turned around grinning at me. I instantly smiled in return. He wrapped his arms around my waist and embraced me.

"You look good as fuck shorty," he said kissing my lips.

"Eww," Gio said from the back seat.

Q and I laughed while he opened the door for me. I climbed into seat and rested my arm on the arm rest. I made sure to bring my pain meds with me just in case. Lately the pain hadn't been that bad and I was able to function a little longer without having to take them. I was finally able to move my shit again and I was thankful for that. Q pulled off and headed toward the expressway.

When we pulled up to his mother's house, I was in awe. Her home was beautiful. Something straight off HGTV. The entire block and in front of her home were filled with cars, most of them foreign. I knew that Q's daddy was a known nigga but damn. There were people also in front of the house talking and laughing. There was one spot left in the winding driveway which must have been reserved for Q. When he pulled in, everyone's eyes immediately shifted to him. Everyone crowded around his Audi saying what's up.

When we stepped out, the loud music immediately flooded my ears.

Shorty what you want? Shorty what you need?
My niggas run the game, we ain't ever leavin'
Countin' up this money, we ain't never sleepin'
You got V12, I got 12 V's
Got bottles, got weed, got molly
I'm all the way up
Shorty what you want? I got what you need
Shorty what you want? I got what you need
Shorty what you want? I got what you need

Q and I walked hand in hand, while Q carried Gio's overgrown butt. Gio was playing shy now that we were around so many unfamiliar faces. We stopped every few steps to speak to Q's family and friends of the family. Once we finally made it to the backyard it was packed with more people. There was a DJ, tables and tables of food, and about three grills still going. His mama went all out for her man. When we walked up the steps to the deck, I instantly became nervous. I knew his mother and father were waiting on the inside. There was even more people on the inside of the house.

When we walked in, Jhalani and Dame were seated at island laughing and talking with who I assumed were Q's parents. Q's father locked eyes with Q and a huge grin spread across his face. The look in their eyes read pure, genuine, unconditional love. Q let my hand go and hugged his father. A few tears welled up in my eyes. His mother was in full fledge tears with a smile on her face. She was just as happy as her boys. After about five minutes they finally let each other go.

"I missed you so much son." His father said.

"I've missed you too old man." Q replied.

His father was handsome as hell. He looked like an older version of Q. He was tall, standing at, at least six five. He had skin the color of peanut butter and piercing brown eyes. His full lips were covered with a beard just like his son. He looked at me and smiled when Q grabbed my hand and pulled me close to him.

"This must be the beauty you've been bragging about," he said staring down at me.

I smiled in return, "Hi, I'm Trinity," I said hugging him as he kissed my cheek in return.

"Nice to meet you beautiful. I'm Capone. Who's this lil guy that's hiding from everybody?"

"That's my son Gio."

After talking with Capone for a few minutes, Q walked me over to his mother who was sipping from a glass of wine. She was beautiful. She embraced Q and kissed his cheek. When she let him go, she walked over to me and embraced me so tightly.

"You must be my future daughter in law."

I smiled, "I'm Trinity and this is my son Gio."

"Just call me, Ma. Aww he's so handsome." she paused and stared at me, "Ahh Q, she's gorgeous. Mama taught you well son."

We all shared a laugh. Jhalani looked at me and smiled. My bff was looking cute today. The glow coming from her was radiant. She was happy, courtesy of her boo Damien. I hadn't seen her this happy in a long time. After talking with Q's parents for a little longer, Jhalani walked over and hugged me. I saw Dame walk over to Q and they excused themselves. Jhalani and I walked over to an empty corner to talk.

"You looking cute today sis," I said to Jhalani with a smile.

"You too. I see you trying to make a good impression on the in laws," she said to me with a smirk.

"You see me?" I laughed. "But damn," I said as I looked around, "Q's daddy knows a lot of people."

"Girl, I said the same thing when we pulled up. But I need to talk you." Jhalani looking in my eyes.

"What's up?" I asked, knowing where this was leading to.

"Sis, I've known you forever. I know how you operate. Do you think we can get past what happened between you and Damien? Please? For me." Jhalani asked with pleading eyes.

I could tell this situation was eating at her in the worst way. I couldn't be the one to make this hard for her. Even though I was still pissed about this damn sling and being shot all together, I had to let it go. What good would it do me to be walking around mad all the time? It was time to let this shit go. Plus, my friend deserved to be happy with no limitations. After all she's been through; I wouldn't make her choose between us.

I sighed, "All is forgiven sis."

Her eyes grew big, "Trini, thank you so much! I swear you don't know how much this shit mean to me. Damien wants to talk to you himself. Q not fucking with him has been stressing him the fuck out." Jhalani laughed slightly.

"Believe me, it's been eating at Q the same way." I said truthfully.

I know Q loves me. I also know that he loves Dame just as much, if not more. I couldn't be the barrier that kept everybody from being happy. We all wanted the same shit. I was feeling much better than I had been and with a few more weeks of consistent therapy, I would be straight in no time. As much as I wanted to be mad, I couldn't. Holding a grudge wouldn't bring me any happiness. Especially if two people I cared about would be affected by it.

I looked up and Gio was walking around with Q's mother as she introduced him to their family. My baby was snuggled up next to her like he'd known her forever.

Q's ma was so sweet and down to earth. Meeting them was easier than I thought it would be. It was so much love in the atmosphere. There were so many people, dancing, talking, and enjoying themselves. I was happy I came. I hadn't had much excitement since my accident. This bbq was lit!

While I sipped on some sangria that Q's ma whipped up for me, I saw Q and Dame coming from the front of the house. Q mouthed 'be nice' to me, when I noticed that Dame was headed in my direction. I gulped down the rest of my drink and sat the glass on the table. Jhalani said she'd be back and headed out the back door of the patio. Dame walked up to me with a nervous look plastered on his face. This shit was awkward as hell for the both of us. All the angry feelings I thought I would have at this moment were replaced with feelings of question. Why didn't he just follow Q's orders? Why didn't he check his surroundings before he let off? I wanted to be mad but, I couldn't. I knew Dame wasn't aiming for me, the 'what ifs' just sent me over the edge.

"Wassup Trini? Can we talk?"

I nodded my head. "Yeah, I think that would be good for the both of us."

We walked over to the living room where it was empty. The entire room was decked out in white and gold décor. As I admired the room, Dame cleared his throat and I walked over and sat on the couch.

Dame laughed and shook his head, "Faye would kill you if she knew you were sitting on that white furniture."

I jumped up, "Shit!"

He laughed again, "I won't say shit," he ran his hand over his face, "Look T, this shit been eating at me heavy. I'm sorry about what happen. I'm sure you know I wasn't trying to hit you. All the possibilities of what could have happened have eaten at me for the last few weeks. I swear on my life, I'm sorry. I don't even know what I would have done if you wasn't able to stand here and hear a nigga out right now. I'm just glad you here and I don't know what else to say but I'm sorry. I know you probably hate a nigga right now but I just hope we can move past this one day."

I sighed, "I can't even sit here and lie to you and act like I wasn't pissed. Before this moment, I didn't know if I would ever forgive you. As much as I wanted to hate you, I can't front and say I do. It's taken me awhile to become ok with this, but I have accepted it and chose to live in the fact that I'm alive. I won't think about the 'what ifs' anymore because they don't count. The fact that I have two people in my life that love you also plays into my forgiveness. So, I'm willing to move forward and try to rebuild our friendship."

Dame smiled and opened up his arms, "I swear to God you don't know how good a nigga feels right now. Can I please have a hug?"

I smiled and hugged him back, "your ass better be at my next therapy session with Q."

He laughed and promised he'd be there. It felt good to finally have this conversation and put this shit behind me. I realized trying to hold a grudge would be pointless. It would take some time to rebuild our relationship but at least we were trying to start somewhere.

QUARAN

My fuckin pops was finally home! After a few years my nigga was finally out that pussy ass FED joint. Mom's threw him this lavish ass barbecue with all the family, his friends, and the niggas that used to run the block with him. I ain't seen my mama so happy in a long time. She has been smiling since I got here. Capone was the only nigga in the world that could tame Faye. Mom's was down for my pops like no other woman could be. Faye was just as gangster as my pops and I think that's why he loved her so much. I craved the type of love my mama had for my father. Shit was so genuine, so pure, and unconditional.

I sat on the deck, sipping from a bottle of Ace of Spades laughing with my father and a few of his buddies. I waited impatiently while Dame had a much needed talk with Trinity. I can't even front like I haven't missed my brother. I'm not used to making moves without him. Chevy and Scooter my niggas a hunnid grand but Dame could never be replaced. I know what happened put a wedge in things but I needed both of them to hash shit out and move forward. My life had become complicated as is and I needed two of the most important people in my life to at least get along. When I looked up and saw them coming out the sliding doors, smiling, my assumptions were confirmed. Knowing that Trinity had put her ill feelings to the side to patch shit up made a nigga happy as hell. She held a special place in my heart. In such a short time, I've grown to love who she is as a person. She holds a nigga down and I fuck with that.

"Aye cuz, that's your bitch?" my cousin Malik asked.

"Watch yo fuckin mouth. Yeah that's my woman. Learn some respect, you don't get a pass because you family lil nigga."

He threw his hands up, "my bad cuz."

"Yeah I know."

I stood up and walked over to Trinity and met her in the middle of the deck. She leaned up and whispered in my ear that she missed me. The DJ had the music blasting and we could barely hear each other. Trinity wrapped her arm around my neck and kissed my lips. Shorty was so affectionate and I loved it. She told me that everything between her and Dame was smooth. I told her I appreciated her for patching shit up. We stood there in the midst of everybody just staring at each other. Trinity bit her lip and kissed me again.

"I love you baby," she told me.

"I love you too shorty."

The DJ was playing some old school ninety's music. Everybody was dancing and having a good ass time. When he played that old R. Kelly, all the older folks got up to dance. He was playing a stepper's song, Step in the Name of Love. My mama walked over to me, trying to step with me. She knew damn well I didn't dance. When she realized I wasn't moving she grabbed Trinity's hand. To my surprise, Trinity knew how to step to. Her and my mama were laughing and stepping their asses off. Trinity was keeping up too, one arm and all. Shorty was full of surprises. With her occupation, I didn't take her for the stepping type at all. I know mom's was going to give me an ear full later. She was definitely feeling Trinity. Mom's has never been this open with any chick I've ever fucked with. Not even my ex. It took her awhile to open to her.

Mom's strutted over to me while Trinity went over to talk to Jhalani and Candice who had just shown up with Chevy. He nodded at me with a smile. Nigga must've had news to share. Mom's walked up, just as my Auntie Sheena did.

"Boy, where you find that big booty ass girl from," Auntie Sheena asked as she leaned against mom's, "I need her doctor."

My mama hit her sister in the arm, "girl shut up, that girl ain't had no surgery," she looked at me, "has she?"

I laughed, "hell naw. Why you hating Auntie? Shorty all natural."

"Mmhm. I don't believe it," my auntie said walking off.

My mama rolled her eyes, "Q, you picked a good one son. I'm proud of you."

My mama hugged me. Chevy walked over with Damien in tow. Mom's excused herself, walking back over to her man. Chevy was grinning from ear to ear.

"What bro? You smashed Candice?" I asked.

"Y'all fucking around?" Dame asked with his eyebrow raised.

Chevy looked at Dame, "yes," then he looked at me and said, "No, but I like her mean ass. Shorty so no nonsense and I love it. She be straight checking my ass."

"Good. You need a bitch like that. You a wild nigga, she perfect for yo ass." Dame said.

I nodded, "I agree with bro. You need to calm yo hot ass down."

"Shorty might be the winner." Chevy said laughing.

My pops called me over and told Chevy and Dame to follow him. We followed him into the house and into his office. A few of the other old heads were already sitting there waiting for us. They were all sitting at the big ass round table inside the office.

My pops cleared his throat and silence fell upon the room, "so I called this quick meeting to clear up a few things. Originally when I left, Q was supposed to take over the operation until I was released. Now that I'm home, I decided to allow my son to keep running things. He's done a great fucking job keeping shit together in my absence. Money is flowing in heavily. Actually more than it was before," he looked at me, "son," he looked at Dame and Chevy, "my other sons. Y'all young niggas have proven to be worthy of running the business. Dame and Chevy I appreciate you two for looking out for my boy while I was gone. I see no reason for me to try and run shit anymore. I'm leaving this shit to you young niggas.

Plus, Faye would be on my ass if she found out I was still trying to run the streets."

Laughter erupted throughout the room.

"Thanks pops. I appreciate the knowledge and shit you gave me. If it wasn't for you, shit wouldn't be running as smooth as it is." I said as my father pulled me into a manly hug.

After he let me go, he hugged Dame and Chevy the same.

Dame, Chevy, and I headed back out to the deck in the back to finish partying. Mom's was outside with the girls popping another bottle of champagne. This time, Trinity's people were outside with them. Terrance, Trinity's father, dapped me up and headed inside to speak to my father.

"Q why didn't you tell me Trinity was Terrance and Lisa's daughter?" Mom's asked.

I shrugged, "my bad ma."

**

"Y'all good?" I asked.

The last of the party had just left. It was three in the morning. Trinity, Jhalani, and Candice had just finished helping my mom straighten up a little bit. Chevy and Dame were taking out the last of the trash. Gio was passed out on the love seat in the sitting area. I was passed tired and damn sure didn't feel like driving back to the crib. Once Chevy and Dame came back in, they left with Jhalani and Sugar.

"Y'all don't have to drive home. Its plenty spare bedrooms around here," my mama said leaning against the kitchen island.

"Yeah, y'all look tired as hell," Capone said wrapping his arms around my mama.

I looked at Trinity and she smiled back and shrugged her shoulders. I walked over to the couch and scooped Gio in my arms. Trinity followed me up the stairs.

"If y'all hear Faye screaming, ignore it." My pops yelled from the kitchen.

I shook my head and Trinity laughed.

"Them niggas nasty."

I stopped in one of the smaller bedrooms and laid Gio in the bed. I took his shoes off and pulled the cover over him. I hit the light switch and grabbed Trinity's hand and led her to my old bedroom. I still had clothes here so I grabbed an old t shirt and tossed it to her. I sat on the edge of the bed and watched her undress. She looked at me then shied away when my stare became too intense. I stood up and helped her pull her dress over arm.

"You in any pain?" I asked.

She shook her head, "nah, I'm ok."

After helping her put the shirt on, I sat down and pulled in her in my lap.

I kissed her neck, "I love you shorty. I appreciate the fuck outta you for coming with me."

She smiled and turned to kiss my lips, "where else would I have been? I love you too."

"Not in my house," my mama said leaning her head in my room and then closing the door.

Trinity and I laughed and she stood up off my lap. She climbed under the cover and stared at me. I looked away. She was too fucking beautiful for me. I had to look away before I disobeyed Faye's rules. I walked over to the door and turned the light off. I climbed in the bed beside Trinity and wrapped my arms around her waist.

"Have you thought about what I asked you?" I asked.

She turned around to face me even though I couldn't see her, "yeah I have."

"And?"

"I'm with it. I don't see why not. I be missing you when you not around and a change of scenery might be good for me."

"Cool. How about I pay off your condo and you can rent it out? It'll be extra money for you." I offered. I mean shit it made sense. If she was gone be staying with me, why not rent the spot out and collect the money for it?

"You serious? You would do that for me?" She asked. I could hear the smile in her voice.

I laughed, "yeah ma. You're mine, I'd do whatever for you."

"Thanks baby."

"I got you Trin, remember that."

**

I blew the Kush smoke into the air while I listened to Dame, Scooter, and Chevy argue over which Instagram bitch looked the best. I shook my head at them. These niggas were dumb as fuck. I couldn't believe they were going back and forth over a couple of bitches who don't even look like themselves. Made up, plastic ass bitches. I would never get hyped up over a chick who goes and get a ton of surgery then wanna act like a bad bitch. I'd take a regular ass chick over a fake bitch any day.

"Q, would you tell these niggas she looks better than her?" Scooter said to me shoving his phone in my face.

I lightly pushed it away, "Nigga, all y'all tripping. Why y'all bugging over fake hoes anyway? Let me see them hoes before the surgery."

Chevy laughed, "Aye bro, get yo ole uptight ass outta here. You know them bitches look good, fake asses and all."

I shook my head while laughing, "Yea, shit all fun and games until you get the bitch pregnant and y'all kids looking like little gremlins."

"Man, you right about that. I never thought it about it like that," Dame said chiming in, "I'd be mad as hell, my daughter come out looking like a muhfucka I never seen."

We all shared a laughed.

"Aye who that?" Chevy asked nodded his head at the car slowing up down the street.

I looked in the direction of where he was looking and instantly became exasperated. When the silver Beemer stopped in front of us, I approached her with a scowl on my face. This bitch was being disrespectful. I didn't even let Trinity come to my spots. I don't know why the fuck Andrea thought she was special. She shifted the car in park and climbed out of the driver's seat. She marched up to me with her arms folded over her chest. This broad had a lot of nerve pulling with an attitude.

"What the fuck are you doing over here?" I asked in a tight voice.

She smiled and then ran her hand down my chest, "I came to see you."

Off impulse, I slapped her hand down.

"Shorty is you off your rocker or what? First thing first, keep yo hands off me, second, why the fuck is you here?"

She chuckled a little bit, "Calm down. Did your girl tell you we met the other day?"

"What? You thought she wasn't? She told me you were being real disrespectful too. Fuck is wrong with you?"

"What's wrong with me?" she asked with her eyes bucked. "Excuse me for not being happy about having to randomly meet your girl. I'm already stressing about this shit going on with you. Then I have to sit across from her pretty ass and act like I'm happy about it? Nah," she said waving her hand.

"Stressed? About what Andrea? Some shit that you brought on yourself. Had you been one hunnid with me from jump, all of this could have been avoided," I paused for a minute, "better yet, I'm glad you fucked up."

Her mouth dropped. I knew that last statement would add insult to injury. I didn't give a fuck. If this bitch wanted to play games, then I'd show her how to play games. Andrea knew better than to fuck with me. She knew I was a humble ass dude, but she also knew that I wasn't the one to play with. If Andrea felt like she wanted to cause me any problems, she knew I wouldn't hesitate to body her ass.

"Bro, you good?" Dame asked nodding his head in Andrea's direction.

I nodded back.

"Fuck you Quaran. Just help me take care of our baby. That's all I care about. It's obvious you ain't trying to fuck with me anymore." She said.

I chuckled a little. Andrea must really take me for some type of lame ass nigga. *Just help her take care of our baby.* This bitch was tripping if she thought I was just about to throw her some money without a DNA test.

"Set up the appointment for the DNA test and then we'll talk."

I turned around and walked back over Chevy and 'nem. I could hear her smack her lips while she climbed back into her car. A few seconds later, I heard her tires scraping the pavement as she pulled off. All the guys were looking confused as hell as I walked up. They all knew my past with Andrea. They were all probably as surprised to see her as I was.

"Where the fuck that bitch come from?" Damien asked firing up another blunt.

Damien had always warned me that Andrea was crazy. He's never liked her and it wasn't until recently that I understood why. I should've taken bro's advice and cut that bitch off back in the day. I wouldn't even be dealing with her craziness right now.

"Dawg, I haven't seen that bitch in forever," Chevy intervened.

"The last time y'all saw that bitch is the last time I saw that bitch." I confirmed.

Scooter laughed, "Damn boss, you can't catch a fucking break."

"Tell me about it," I replied.

I shook my head. He was right. The situation with Geno was slowly coming to a head. I had Chevy still keeping in contact with that shady bitch Jade. She was still pillow talking with the nigga, spreading their business and hers. I needed to take care of the situation pronto because he was becoming annoyed with shorty. Nigga was all in his feelings because he was feeling Candice and he didn't want her thinking he was on some shady shit. I understood. But until this situation was handled, I needed him to play his part.

After we finished smoking, we headed in to count up the drop offs that were made today. Business was booming for me. I had the finest of everything; and for that very reason I had niggas copping weight from me. I wasn't the plug, but I was damn sure close. My father fucked with these Italian dudes that started to supply me while pops was gone. They fucked with me heavy off the strength of my father. They wouldn't supply any other nigga in the city besides me. The more they flooded me with work, the more niggas came at me wanting to buy.

Like I stated before, I hadn't done this beef shit in a while; years to be exact. I was too old and too focused on other shit. The need to get out this dope game was weighing heavy on me. I wanted regular shit like a wife and kids. This dope game wasn't shit I wanted to do for the rest of my life. That's why I was trying to put my hands in as much shit as I could. I was working on buying a few properties, a few commercial and a few to rent out.

Shit was all in the works, I just needed to carefully plan and execute.

JHALANI

"Jhalani, I'm about to go to the grocery store. Be back in a few," my mom yelled up the stairs.

"Ok."

I was standing in the full length mirror, fluffing up my Auburn curls. I was about to head out and meet up with Sasha. I needed the scoop on her brother. My nerves wouldn't be put to rest unless I knew what was going on with him. Hopefully by now she had heard something from him. The stress was killing me. My weight had dropped tremendously. Thank God my hair hadn't fallen out. The unknown bothered the fuck out of me. When I hit her up wanting to meet, she happily obliged. She still looked at me like a sister and I appreciated her for looking out.

She frequently called and texted to check up on me. I didn't tell her about the blocked texts and calls I had been receiving. I wanted to save that for our lunch date. I prayed that she had some good news to tell me. Hopefully something like the nigga has moved out of town or something. Tuh! That would be too farfetched. I shook my feelings of uneasiness and grabbed my shoes.

I slid my feet into my sandals and tied them up. I gave myself the once over and grabbed my keys and purse.

I sped all the way to Mexican restaurant we were meeting at. Not only was I starving but I needed a margarita.

When I pulled up, I parked and went inside. I looked around the packed restaurant until I spotted her sitting in the corner. She flashed me her perfect smile and waved. When I made to the back, I slid my purse in the booth and hugged her. Just as I sat down the waitress came over and took our drink orders.

"Sooo, how are you? Sasha asked.

I sighed, "I'm living boo, but I'm stressed the fuck out," I answered truthfully.

"What's going on?" she asked stuffing her phone in her purse.

I ran down everything to her about the calls and text messages. I even told her that I didn't even feel safe anywhere because of it. Tears cascaded down my eyes as I vented to her. Every emotion I had been feeling came out. The hurt, the anger, the fear, just everything I had been experiencing was all hitting me at once. I had been keeping my feelings bottled up trying to be strong for everyone else. Between being there for Trinity and making sure Dame was good, I hadn't taken any time for myself.

"Lani, why didn't you tell me? You thought it was Miles?" she asked handing me a napkin to wipe my face.

"I mean, who else would it be?"

She shrugged, "I don't know. I get why you think that. I just don't think it's him. He's been going to counseling and has even gone to rehab for his drinking.

The other day he brought some girl home that I guess he's seeing now," she replied.

"Really?" I asked a little shocked.

"Yeah. He said that they met at counseling and she's been helping him get back on track. He seems like he's trying to change Lani. He even started a new job."

I don't know why, but that information stung a little. I know I shouldn't care but I couldn't deny the tinge of jealousy I felt. All the years I invested in him and he wants to change after we break up. What kind of shit is that? I spent so much time trying to get him to change and go get help. Wait! Why do I care so much? I had a nigga that loved me and a great support system. I shouldn't be tripping over what he's doing, right? The last few months I spent with him were pure hell. But the years of bliss we spent together outshined those. Ugh! I need to shake these feelings. I came here in hopes of him doing something with himself, why the fuck am I so pressed?

"Wow, that's good." I mumbled.

I needed to get out of my feelings. I was tripping over nothing. Here I was thinking about the past when I should have been embracing the future. Miles put me through a lot over the last few months we shared together. I should be celebrating the fact that he has changed and moved on but I can't shake the jealousy I feel. Why wasn't I worthy enough for him to change? If he would have done right by me, we would have been getting ready to have a baby. We'd be celebrating the one of the happiest moments in our lives. Instead, he was getting his shit together and trying to build with someone else.

"Are you okay boo?" Sasha asked as the waitress sat our drinks at the table.

I took a sip of my margarita and shook my head up and down. The waitress asked for our food orders as I skimmed over the menu. After Sasha placed her order, I placed mine. My appetite was shot now. I was tripping hard and it was annoying me. I thought I was over Miles.

I looked up and Sasha was staring at me.

"What?" I asked.

"You sure you okay? You look like something is bothering you."

"Am I wrong for feeling a tinge of jealousy?" I asked Sasha as I stared at her with question.

She smiled, "Girl no. I understand. You and my brother have history. I know he put you through a lot but its normal to miss the good times. Just keep moving forward Lani. Y'all served a purpose in each other's lives and that purpose is filled."

In a sense she was right. I needed to go let go of what could have been. If it was meant to be then we would be together. I took a deep breath and relaxed. I needed to embrace what was right in my life. The thought of how foolish I would look trying to have a relationship with Miles made me cringe. I would look like a complete fool taking him back after all he put me through.

**

"You like this corny ass shit?"

I looked up at Damien who was watching me sing along to Drake's new song Controlla, "Yeah. This is my shit. You're tripping if you don't like it."

"You tripping if you think it's a hit," Dame replied turning off his Beats pill.

"Damn, you're a hater."

I was standing in the mirror of his master bathroom applying my makeup. I was getting ready for work. It was Thirsty Thursday which meant it was going to be a busy night for me. Damien, along with Q and Trinity were coming to tip their favorite bartender. I was surprised at Trinity coming out because of her sling. I guess my boo was growing up. I remember a time where she wouldn't leave the house if she was on her period.

Damien walked up behind me and wrapped his arms around me, "Why you caking all that shit up on your face? You don't even need it."

My lips curled up into a smile, "thanks baby. I wear it because I like it."

I turned around and wrapped my arms around his neck. I stood on the tip of my toes and placed a soft kiss on his lips. He tightened his grip around my waist and intensified the kiss. I lightly sucked on his bottom lip. His lips were the softest. He moved his hands down to my ass where he gripped firmly. He traced his kisses to my neck where he began to suck lightly. I moaned as little as my middle began to moisten.

I hissed, "Daaame, stop," I whined, "You're going to make me late for work."

"So fucking what," he said as I eased out of his grip.

"Later, ok?" I said biting my bottom lip.

He nodded, "Ima hold you to that shit."

An hour later we were pulling up to the club. The lot was packed with cars and people mingling and waiting to get in. I climbed out of the car and I immediately began rubbing my arms. The weather was changing and the booty shorts and referee shirt I wore was hardly keeping me warm. My long socks were already as far up my leg as they would go. I shivered a little as I trudged inside the club. It was still kind of early and it was already live. Some of the girls were already walking around with bags full of money.

I went and checked in with Moonie while Damien went and sat with Trinity, Q and Chevy. I was eager to make some money tonight. My savings was dwindling down and I needed to build it back up. I wanted to move out of my parent's house soon and I needed my cash to be on point. After checking my appearance, I headed back to the bar.

It was crowded and the other two bartenders looked overwhelmed. I shook my head. Both of the girls were new. I stepped behind the bar and immediately began taking orders. In a matter of minutes most of the crowd was cleared. I scanned over the crowd while I grabbed change for a customer. My eyes landed on Damien who was staring at me smiling. My lips instantly curled up. He was so damn silly. The more I stared at him, I realized how much I was tripping earlier. This man fucked with me heavy and I had the nerve to be upset about the past. I shook my head at myself and walked back over to my customer.

I heard someone calling my name and looked to my left. Candice's crazy ass was waving me over with Trinity standing beside her.

"Hey sis," Trinity said while laughing at Candice.

"Hey boo," I replied, "what the hell you want Candice?"

"Girl I need a fucking drink. Don't you see Chevy sitting over there eyeballing me and shit, ugh," Candice said tossing me a twenty, "Henny straight, please boo."

"Hold up bish! I know you not intimidated by Chevy. Not yo extra confident ass." I said with my hands on my hips.

"I said the same shit sis," Trinity said, "bitch nervous as hell. Talking about she needs a drink, girl bye."

Candice cocked her head to the side, "Trinity, I know damn well you ain't talking."

Trinity waved her off, "Aye we're not talking about me. This is about you."

I walked off shaking my head and grabbed Candice her Henny. It was funny seeing Candice all nervous over a nigga. She was usually the confident, go getter type. But I guess since she's gotta dance tonight, it's a different setting than outside the club. I took Candice her drink and finished helping out the customers.

It was almost two in the morning and I was tired as fuck. Trinity and Q had left already. My boo was still sitting in the back waiting for me with Chevy. I know he's tired as fuck and ready to go. I appreciated him for coming out with me tonight. I watched as Candice and Chevy flirted while she danced for him. They were so cute together. I always thought that friends who dated friends was corny as hell but hey I guess that's the way shit happens sometimes.

"Aye Tamika, I'm about to go to the bathroom, be right back." I said to the new bartender.

I stepped from behind the bar and headed to the back of the club. I wiped my hands on the back of my shorts as I maneuvered through the thick crowd. I spoke to a couple of the regulars as they got dances and sipped from their drinks. I know Moonie makes a killing off these people. All the dope boys, credit card scammers, and even the niggas with legit jobs stay coming through here to spend their money. He even had some of the finest women in Chicago working for him. Niggas were suckers for a pretty face.

I turned the corner for the bathroom when I was grabbed from behind and pulled into the men's bathroom. Panic instantly took over my body. I was trying to scream but my mouth was covered. I began to try to fight but whoever it was had a grip on me.

"Shh, shh! Calm down Lani, it's just me."

I turned around and looked at him in disbelief. His hair was freshly cut and his facial hair nicely lined up. He had on new clothes and a freshly bought pair of Jordan's. I hated to even admit it but he looked good. Damned good. Miles looked at me with fear. He wasn't sure how I was going to react. I was scared, I couldn't front. I hadn't seen this nigga in months. I didn't know what to expect. We both just stood there staring at each other. My chest heaved up and down as I tried to calm down. I couldn't believe that I was standing face to face with this nigga.

He threw his hands up, "Lani look, I'm not here on bullshit. Just give me a few minutes of your time."

I nodded my head as I stood in the corner of the bathroom with my arms wrapped around me.

He exhaled and stuffed his hands into the pockets of his jeans, "Jhalani, I am so sorry for all the shit I put you through. I talked to Sasha today and she told me y'all had been talking. She told me about the texts and shit that you were receiving. She does not know it was me but it was. I'm sorry. I've seen you out a few times with yo new nigga and it had me fucked up. I realize the reason you were forced to move on was because of my fuck ups. After this, I swear I won't bother you anymore. I should have appreciated you when I had the chance. Because of you, I've been trying to get my shit together. I've stopped drinking and even found me job. I just want to thank you for pushing me to do better. I'll always love you baby girl, even if you never talk to me again."

He walked up to me and I tensed up. He placed a soft kiss on my forehead and walked toward the bathroom door. He turned around to face me and just stared for a minute.

"I hope dude treating you right and that you get everything you deserve."

He turned around and walked out of the bathroom. I stood there confused as hell. What the fuck just happened?

TRINITY

"Girl, he took me out last night. I had a ball."

I sat in the chair at the nail shop getting a pedicure with Tavia. She was currently telling me about her new love interest. Finally, my little baby found her somebody to give her time to. Tavia was only twenty-two but she had an old soul. She wanted what every girl wanted, except she wasn't out here like a lot of girls her age were. I hoped that whatever guy she was dealing with was worth it.

"Where did y'all go?" I asked looking through the swatches of the no-chip polish.

"We went to Eddie V's. The food was so fucking good." Tavia boasted.

"Damn, he's putting in work huh? He ain't the typical *let's chill* type of nigga either, you might have a winner sis," I said to Tavia as I passed the swatches to the young, mocha colored girl that was doing my pedicure.

"I hope so sis. A bitch tired of these young immature ass niggas out here. I know I'm young, but shit I know what I want," Tavia said relaxing into the comfortable recliner.

"I know. Just stay on alert for any fuck shit. He seems like good dude but until you've figured him all the way out, just let it flow."

"Oh believe me, I am," Tavia said scrolling through her phone.

It had been a few weeks since being shot and I was feeling so much better. I had been coming out of the house much more than before. My wound had healed and tomorrow I was getting out of this sling. A bitch was ecstatic, ya hear me? Over a month in this sling was pure torture. The wait was finally over and I could finally get back to my old self. Doing simple things had become a hassle and very frustrating but the way Q had been catering to me, I didn't miss a beat. I was in love with that man like no other. He was like heaven sent or some shit.

We had slowly begun packing up my place so that I could move in with him. I decided to let Candice and her boys move into my place so that she could be in a safer neighborhood. I trusted her to take care of my shit and she was reliable. I knew my spot would be in good hands. Her lease was up in a month and that gave me a small amount of time to pack up. I couldn't wait until this moving shit was over. I was excited to be moving in with Q, but the whole process annoyed me.

My parents thought everything was happening kind of fast but they liked him and I loved him. It's been about eight months and so much has happened. Every single thing we've been through has brought us closer together. I'd be a fool to try and stop what was happening. I had been praying for a man like Q and now it was time to enjoy it.

The dinging of the door caused me to look up. Geno's other baby mama was walking in the shop with her ratchet ass sister in tow. The bitch must have had her baby because she wasn't pregnant. She still had a small pudge and had the nerve to have on a damn crop top. I rolled my eyes at them. Funky ass bitches. If I didn't have this damn sling on, I'd probably get up beat that ass again. Tavia took her attention off the nail tech and looked at me. She raised her eyebrows as a way of asking was I ok. I mouthed 'I'm good' and relaxed in my chair.

I felt someone invading my space so I looked up. Geno's baby mama was sitting next to me. Instantly I went into defense mode. If I had to, I would beat this bitch's ass one hand and all.

"Calm down honey, ain't nobody tryna beef with you," she said as she rolled her eyes.

I smacked my lips, "then what the fuck do you want?"

"Our kids are siblings; I think they should get to know each other."

Was this bitch crazy or what? Did she really think that I would be open to that? For starters, I don't even like this bitch or her sister. Secondly, Geno has proven to me over and over why I don't want my son around him. Third, did she really think that I wanted my son around her ratchet ass or that I wanted to be around her kid? Nah, not even. Her and Geno could have each other and play house all they wanted to. Gio was not going to be a part of it.

"Girl please, my son is good. He doesn't need you, your child, or his weak ass daddy. We don't fuck with y'all," I said standing as I watched Tavia walked over to us.

Tavia walked over with a mug.

"Everything good over here?" she asked.

"Aint shit poppin off sis. I'm *good*," I said putting emphasis on good as I walked by mugging Strawberry who was standing off to the side.

"Mm, how's that arm?" Geno's baby mom laughed as I was about to exit the shop.

"Great, bitch. You wanna see if I still have my strength?"

"It's cool lil baby, we'll meet again. Believe that," she said smirking.

Her last statement didn't sit right with me. I felt like the bitch was making a threat. If it wasn't for Tavia pushing me through the door and to her car, I probably would have tried to hit her. Tavia was rapping to me about being a woman and letting that rat be a rat. She was right in a sense but I did not tolerate disrespect. Especially from a bird bitch. I was fuming as we climbed inside Tavia's car. The nerve of that bitch.

**

"You should've smacked her disrespectful ass, ugh. Why don't shit ever pop off when I'm around?" Candice asked smacking on some chili fries.

"Because God knows you a nutcase, that's why," Jhalani said taking a fry from Candice's plate.

I laughed, shaking my head at them. I was currently sitting at my dining room table eating food that they had brought me. I was in a zone, mind racing with a million thoughts. I was so sick of these bitches. I didn't even deal with Geno anymore and was still dealing with the bullshit attached to him. He was always drama and I see nothing has changed.

"Do Jade still hang with them messy hoes? I haven't seen her with them in a minute," I asked sipping from my Pepsi.

Candice shrugged, "I have no idea. But I do know that Chevy been keeping tabs on the bitch for Q."

I rose my eyebrow, "What?"

"Apparently the bitch been keeping tabs on them for Chevy. But the info is for Q. I guess them hoes fell out. Jade been spilling all the tea." Candice said.

"Oh so you figured out why that bitch was blowing up his phone?" I asked.

"Yeah, I had to ask. I couldn't even ignore the fact that she was constantly calling. I thought he was fucking with her but he checked my ass." Candice said.

"I just don't get what Geno's deal is. Damn, let me fuckin live." I said throwing my hands up.

"Girl, Geno been on one ever since you started fucking with Q. His ole mad ass. Ugh, I could never stand that nigga," Jhalani said pointed her fork at me, "he's bitter and jealous because he ain't running shit like he used to."

"He's always been the jealous type. That ain't Q's fault. He's so ugh! Why do he gotta fuck with what I have going on? I haven't bothered Geno's bitter ass in years." I said.

My phone rang interrupting our conversation.

I looked down at the screen and rolled my eyes. *Speak of the fucking devil.* I snatched up the phone and slid the green button over. I pressed the speaker so that Jhalani and Candice could listen.

"What nigga?" I asked.

"Damn, so harsh. What just happened with you and my bm?" Geno asked.

"Nigga what? Aint shit just happen. The bitch started talking crazy and I checked her ass, nothing major."

Did this nigga really just call me, trying to check me over his wack ass bm?

"Well that ain't what she said. She said you popped off with her. I know you and your attitude so it's believable." Geno said like he had an attitude.

"Fuck you and that bitch. I don't give a fuck what she told you. She's a liar and your retarded ass believe anything she say," I spat angrily.

"That's why I don't fuck with you now," he yelled.

"Wow, you really think I give a fuck?" I laughed, "When has your presence ever made a difference in mine or Gio's life?"

He was silent.

"Exactly!" I yelled at the phone.

"Fuck you and Gio," he yelled before hanging up in my face.

The fact that he said fuck me, didn't bother me one bit. The fact that his own son's name came out of his mouth left me stuck. What type of man says that about his own child? Tears welled up in my eyes. Not because I was hurt, but because I was furious. My hands were shaking I was so upset. Jhalani and Candice walked over to me and hugged me as the tears fell freely. If I ever ran across Geno again, I'd kill that mothafucka myself.

**

A month later.

It was officially Fall and I was all moved into Q's big ass house. Well, *our* big ass house. Funny how we met in Spring and look at us now. I never expected for shit to move this fast but I'm not complaining. Q said if we were going to do this, then let's go all the way. Why wait around years to make shit happen? I had never moved this fast with anyone but I liked the feeling of having a man that loved me fully. Most of the time, when you move slow and take your time, shit doesn't work out anyway. Why not go all in?

Shit had been real quiet for the last month and I was worried. I've enjoyed every minute of not having to deal with any drama. But really, how long does that last? I was finally back one hundred percent with my injury and had started working again. Q wasn't happy about that at all. He constantly stressed to me that I didn't have to work, but I wasn't that girl. I could never sit on my ass and let a man take care of me and I not contribute. My savings was steady building up and my bank account was looking real nice. Q wouldn't accept any money from me on the bills either. So I went behind his ass back and paid a few without him knowing. He'd curse my ass out when he did find out.

Currently, I was sitting at the vanity he bought me, doing my makeup. I was getting ready for work. I didn't want to do all that at the club so I did what I could at home. I heard Q's heavy ass footsteps coming up the stairs. I already knew what to expect when he saw me. I stood up and grabbed my PINK joggers off the bed and slipped my legs in.

"Where you headed?" Q asked grabbing a hand full of my ass before I could pull my pants all the way up.

"Uh, work..."

He sighed and pulled me into him, "why shorty?"

I turned around to face him and wrapped my arms around his neck, "Because I have to make my money baby."

"How many times I gotta tell you, you good?"

I sighed, "Q, I understand that. But can you let me make my own money?"

"T, come on now. It's other ways you can make money. A nigga didn't mind at first, but you mine now. I don't want all these niggas knowing what you got."

I sighed, "aight bae, look, will you at least give me til the beginning of the year? That's two months away."

He stared off for a second before reluctantly shaking his head 'yes', "Aight Trini, I'm giving you until New Years Eve. After that, this shit over. You too damn smart wasting yo fucking time in a strip club."

I smirked, "ok Daddy."

"Yeah aight."

As much as I loved making this money, I couldn't even lie and say I was upset about quitting. I had two months to come up with my next move. I couldn't go work at a regular nine to five, I needed my own business. I really wanted to open up a store, so maybe that's what my next venture should be. I needed something that I would enjoy and that would make me some coins. As for now, I needed to hustle up the rest of my money to add to my savings. I know that Q was dead ass about me quitting and he wouldn't let up on our decision.

When I pulled up to the club, as usual, it was packed out. People were everywhere. Tonight was special because it was Moonie's birthday. The whole city came out to show love. Tonight would be one for the books. There was a lot of money to be made tonight and I was about to work the hell out of this stage.

I made my way to the back and found Candice. The back room was hectic. There was so much chaos from all the girls running around trying to look their best and get themselves together. I walked up to her and she was talking privately with Jade in the back corner. Candice wore a mug on her face and instantly I knew something was up.

"What's wrong boo?" I asked looking back and forth between her and Jade.

Candice sighed and looked at Jade, "there she is. Now tell her."

Jade looked like she had seen a ghost. She had fear written on her face and her hands were trembling, "I uh... I was just...just telling Candice," she stuttered, then took a deep breath, "Geno and his bm plotting on you. Please be careful."

I looked at her confusedly, "Jade what are you talking about?"

She looked at me with concern, then looked around, "Trinity please just listen to me. I'm not supposed to say anything. Just take my word and steer clear of them."

Before I could say anything else, she grabbed her bag and ran out the door.

I looked at Candice, "What the fuck was that about?"

Candice shrugged her shoulders and said, "I have no idea. She came up to me all frantic asking could we talk. When I asked her what was up, she started begging me to tell you to stay away from Geno."

"I haven't heard from him in weeks. The last time was that day you and Jhalani were at the crib. Nothing since then." I said stuffing my bag in my locker.

"Well that bitch looked pretty damn serious to me. Just take heed friend and watch your surroundings," Candice said as finished getting dressed.

"I am."

After I finished getting dressed Candice and I hit the floor. I was making money but I couldn't even focus. What Jade had said to me earlier was on my mind heavy. She looked like she was afraid for her own life so I didn't think she was lying. Why though? I haven't done shit to Geno. Why was he gunning for me so hard? Ever since he said fuck me and my son, I had blocked his ass from all forms of communication. Since we had moved in with Q, he didn't even know where we were staying. I planned to keep it that way. I was done playing childish ass games with his immature ass.

"Trini, you good sis?" Jhalani was standing in front of me with her head cocked to the side.

"Yeah, I'm good," I said, "Can I get a bottle of water please?"

She handed me the water and I headed upstairs to Q's section. Even after he fussed at me for coming, he still showed up to 'watch over me' as he says. I knew better though. His ass was here to make sure I wasn't on shit, even though he knew I didn't get down like that. It was cool though, I felt safer with him here. When he spotted me, he smiled and patted his lap. I smiled back and switched over to him. I sat in his lap and he wrapped his arms around my waist.

"What's wrong shorty?" he asked as I rested my head on his shoulder.

"It's nothing," I replied.

He lifted my face chin with his index finger, "Stop lying to me T. What's good?"

"I ran into Jade earlier, she was all in a panic and shit. She told me Geno and his bm been plotting on me."

Q stared at me for a second and then looked off. He was visibly pissed.

"Don't worry about it. I got you." He said before kissing my cheek.

"I know."

"Trust me Trini, I got you."

DAME

"You sure Q knows you doing outside deals my nigga?"

I looked over at Scooter who was sitting in the passenger seat of my whip. Fuck he mean? I'm my own fucking man around this bitch. Besides, Q didn't give a fuck. He was trying to get out the game and I was impatiently waiting for my moment. I was working on building this empire and expansion. True enough, we were making mad money out here in these streets but you could never have enough cheese. There was always money to be made and I was trying to get it by any means. I had been quiet as hell for the last few months, planning my come up. I was already in a set position to make moves thanks to Q and Capone. From doing business with them these last few years, I had built great relationships with some made mothafuckas.

"Yeah nigga. Q getting ready to leave the game anyway, I'm next up."

I thumped my blunt in the ashtray and told Scooter to get out. I didn't like the way he was questioning me. That could become a problem for me later. I wasn't trying to push bro out the way but I was ready to run shit my way. I was tired of running shit by him. Bro was too laid back for me. The way he's handling that shit with Geno is beyond me. By now, I would have so much blood shed around this city. He let Geno get away with doing too much. I would have been peeled that nigga's scalp back. He would have been a dead man already if it wasn't for Trinity being over his crib that day.

Had it not been for her, those bullets would have rained all over that crib.

I was salty as fuck when shorty walked out that front door. I knew what type of treatment I was in when I saw the look on Q's face. At that moment in time, he probably wanted my head more than the nigga he was gunning for. I was happy as hell when he hit me up wanting to talk. I understood where he was coming from. He was definitely feeling Trinity and I hadn't seen that nigga this open with anyone in years. Not even that nutty ass broad Andrea. Trinity must have been special because he had moved her and her son into his crib. I respected it. Real shit was hard to come by these days.

I pulled from in front of one of our spots and headed to Jhalani's crib. Me and shorty had been kicking it real tough, but lately she had been acting differently. I don't know what it is but I wasn't feeling it. We were about to go to dinner and I made a mental note to ask her what was going on. Our friendship was special to me and I didn't want to ruin it over some fuck shit. We needed to discuss whatever was going on with her. If she was having a change of heart, I needed to know.

When I pulled up to her crib, I called her and told her I was outside. I lit another blunt while I waited. We were about to head to Wildfire and I needed my appetite. Shorty liked all that expensive shit. She said that we hadn't been on an official date and she was right. Besides kicking it and doing little shit, we had never been on a real date. If it was going to make her happy, then I was all for it.

I stared at the fiery red tip as I exhaled the smoke into the air. I heard a soft knock on the passenger side window and shorty was standing there looking immaculate. When she climbed in, the Gucci perfume she wore instantly filled the atmosphere. Her long brown hair hung in curls over her shoulders. Shorty even had her makeup done, looking like some runway model. I licked my lips as I admired her curves in the black dress she wore.

"Damn," I mumbled under my breath, "you look good as fuck baby."

She smiled and leaned over with puckered lips, and then she softly kissed mine, "Thanks boo. Where are we going again?"

"Wildfire. That's what you wanted right?" I asked pulling from in front on her crib.

**

"Boy please, I am not pushing five babies out of here," Jhalani said sipping from the glass of wine she ordered.

"Why not? If I wanted five kids, you wouldn't give them to me?" I asked.

She laughed, "No Damien. Three is the max. I'd go crazy with five damn kids."

"Yeah you're saying that now. Until that pipe get in you."

She covered her mouth so that she wouldn't spit out her drink. Once she swallowed she said, "Boy hush."

We had enjoyed our food and were sitting here enjoying each other's company. I stared at her, admiring her beauty. When she glanced down at her phone again, I became a little annoyed. She had been checking her phone all night, texting back and forth with someone. Whoever was texting her, had her full attention. She was conversing with me but obviously her mind was elsewhere.

"Jhalani, what's up? You got something on your mind shorty?" I asked sipping from the glass of water in front of me. I watched her as I sat patiently awaiting an answer.

She tucked a piece of hair behind her ear, "Yea, I do actually. Promise not to get upset?"

I nodded but I couldn't promise her that. It all depended on what she had to say. She knew my temper was a little off the chain. I was working on getting that under control but being a hot head was just in my blood. It was who I was. My temper saved me from a lot of dangerous situations. Acting on impulse it what put a few niggas on the wrong side of the dirt and kept me on the up and up.

She sighed, "I ran into Miles a few days ago."

I looked at her and shrugged, "What that mean shorty? You straight?"

She nodded her head, "Yea, he actually apologized to me. For everything," she cleared her throat, "He's even gone to counseling and gotten his shit together."

"Good for him. What's that gotta do with you though?" I asked.

"I mean, nothing really. I just thought it was a nice gesture. It meant a lot to me after all the shit he's put me through."

Something told me shorty was feeling some type of way over the nigga. I've seen enough of these types of situations to know what shorty was thinking. She was on some reminiscent type shit and I wasn't feeling it. She could sit in front of me and act unfazed all she wanted, but I knew the deal. I wasn't going to overreact though. She had history with dude and I respect that. What I wasn't going to tolerate was her thinking it was cool to text the nigga while she was with me. I could bet my last dollar that, that's who's had her attention all night. Whatever game this nigga was spitting to her had her going. I loved Jhalani but I wasn't a lame nigga by far. I wouldn't let her or any woman for that matter ever treat me as such either.

"So what you saying ma? You ready to dab back into a relationship with this nigga because of a weak ass apology?"

"No Damien, chill."

"Is that who you've been texting all night?" I asked already knowing the answer.

She took a deep breath and stared at me. We both sat there unmoving.

The she opened her mouth and put her head down, "yes."

I didn't even know what to say. What was I supposed to say? Shorty didn't know what to do with herself. She sat there fidgeting while I just watched her. I would never understand how she could sit there and chop it up with a nigga that put her through hell. Did all that fighting just to get away from a nigga, to go right back. I can't even lie, I felt like shit. Sitting here with her and she happily enjoying this fuck nigga's conversation. I thought we were moving forward and she let this nigga come right back and take her from me.

She reached for my hand and I moved it, "Damien, please don't be mad at me. It's not what you think. I just needed some closure. We just got cool, that's it."

"Shorty I can't even fuck with you while you think it's ok for you to be cool with him. It's all good," I said as I waived our waiter over.

When he brought the bill, I paid it and we left. Our ride to her crib was silent. She sat in the passenger seat of my whip with her head down, fidgeting with her nails. I glanced at her and shook my head. How could shorty be so dumb? I'd most definitely be there for her if she ever needed me but she had to see fault in what she was doing. She was playing with fire and when you play fire, you definitely get burned.

**

"Hey baby," she cooed as she fumbled with the button on my jeans.

Since my night was ruined with Jhalani, I had to go with the next best thing. When I called shorty up, she was hot and ready for me, just as she had always been. I used my free hand to grip her ass through her booty shorts as I locked her front door. No matter what or who I was dealing with, shorty kept me on speed dial. She was down to do whatever, whenever I wanted her to. I know what you thinking. How this nigga gone talk shit about Jhalani when he got his own hoes? Nah, it ain't even like that. This bitch was only around when I wanted her to be. Thing is, I was ready to cut her off for Jhalani. But fuck it, it is what it is.

"Slow down Drea, damn," I said as she kissed all over my neck.

She wouldn't even let me get in the door good. She kissed me again before letting me go. She smiled and asked me was I good. I told her that I had a shitty night and was in need of her good ass pussy to make me feel better. Again, I know you tripping over who I'm with right? Aye shorty might be a little nutty but her pussy A1.

"Where you been? I haven't seen you in a few weeks. You were acting funny the last time I saw you." She said sitting a glass of Henny in front of me.

I took a sip and looked at her, "What you wanted me to do Andrea? Q doesn't know I'm fucking with you. We couldn't be obvious. Then he would know something was up." I said.

When I started fucking Andrea, it was an accident. We were both on some drunk shit one night and it ended up happening. I mean shorty is bad as fuck, what man could turn that down? After that night, it became a casual thing and eventually she became pregnant. We both knew the baby was mine and that's why she left town. We were both trying to keep it from Q. At the time, he was fucking with shorty heavy as hell and he'd kill both of us if he found out. I made Andrea leave and set her up in a crib ducked off in Atlanta. Far away from Q as possible. Now she was back as only a distraction to keep Q on his toes. She'd been quiet for a minute and that was because I was trying to enjoy my daughter.

"But fuck him. I deserve to be happy to. He's moved on with that other bitch and he don't even pay me any mind," she said pouting.

I shook my head at her craziness, "Ma, did you forget this is all a game? All you were supposed to do was be a distraction while I make these moves." I asked and she nodded her head no, "Have you told him anything else about *my* daughter?

"No Damien. I haven't even brought it up. I never even went through with the DNA test. And I'm sorry, just seeing him brought back old feelings, I'm good though. You forgive me?" she asked straddling me.

I gripped her ass through her shorts, "Nah, show me how sorry you are."

I threw my head back when she climbed in between my legs and released my dick from my boxers.

This is why this I fucked with this bitch, her sex was A1. On top of that, she was loyal as fuck to me. Andrea was down to do whatever I needed her to do. Helping me distract Q was one of them. Q was my nigga but I needed him to hurry up and leave the dope game. Bro had made a lot of money in these streets and he was ready to dip. Me on the other hand, I was a greedy nigga. I knew the moment he walked away from the game, it was mine. I wanted to expand beyond the blocks we had. I needed the whole city to the burbs under my belt. I wanted it all. While my accounts were looking nice, there was always more money to be made. I was out to take everything, even if that meant knocking a couple niggas off in the process.

JHALANI

When I got in the crib, I felt like straight shit. How could I be so stupid? I knew I was dead ass wrong for texting Miles, especially while I was on a date with Damien. What was this hold that Miles had on me so suddenly? I had gone from trying to get over him to not being able to let go. I felt like a straight up fool for being so naïve, but I couldn't help it. After he left the club that night, I didn't know how to feel about his apology. I thought about it for days after. When I texted him, he was eager to talk. I asked him why he did all the things he did to me. His explanation was simply, depression and anger. I wanted to let go of what we shared, but I'd be a liar if I said the love was gone. For so long, all I ever wanted was for him to get his shit together and make me happy.

Our texts became more frequent and though a little voice kept warning me to stay away, I couldn't. Even tonight, when I knew Damien should have had my undivided attention, I was busy into my conversation with Miles. He was asking me about possibly meeting up soon for dinner but I wasn't sure if I was ready for that yet. Talking to him brought back memories of the way he used to make me feel back in the day. Back when he kept me on my toes and kept a smile on my face.

I sat on my bed, staring at our conversation. When I realized Damien hadn't called or texted me, I knew he was pissed at me. I didn't want to ruin our friendship over my indecisiveness. I knew Damien didn't deserve what I was doing to him, especially after he was the one to rescue me from my messed up situation. He had listened to me vent and talk so much shit about Miles and now look at me. I shook my head at myself and decided to try to call him and apologize.

The phone rung until his automated voicemail picked up. I left a message.

"Damien, it's me. I'm so sorry about tonight. I hope we can talk about this and move past this. I don't want to ruin our friendship. Call me back, please."

I hung up the phone and laid back on my bed.

I just didn't understand where these old feelings were coming from. I had been doing good getting over him and he pops back up into my life. My feelings were all over the place. Confusion was at an all-time high right now. I knew I had no business feeling like this but I what could do? My heart and my mind were in a battle of tug of war and I was being pulled in two different directions. Shit was just crazy.

**

The next morning when I got up, I had the worst headache. I sluggishly got out of bed and walked over to open my drapes. I let the bright sun illuminate my room to bring some light to my shitty mood. I stood in the window for a minute just watching the quietness of the neighborhood. I stretched and walked over to my closet and stared at the ridiculous amounts of clothes that I needed to wash. I sighed and rummaged through the closet until I found a simple Nike tracksuit to throw on. I had a few errands to run and I was supposed to meet with Miles later. I know, I know. I keep saying how upset I am about Damien but I felt like I needed this. We agreed to meet up in a public place but private enough to not run into any of my friends.

I didn't want Trinity to know about this at all. She'd let me have it if she found out and I'd never hear the end of it. I wouldn't dare tell my parents that I was going to meet up with him. My father would try to put hands on him and my mom would flip. This was just going to be private little dinner between the two of us to sort things out. I needed to see for myself what things would have been like if we would have worked out.

After I got myself ready, I headed out the crib. It was nice as hell out and I was feeling a little better after my shower. I was still extremely tired though and I couldn't understand why. My first stop was my doctor's appointment. When I pulled up it wasn't as packed as I expected it to be. I signed in and waited to be called to the back. I sat down in an empty seat in the corner and watched the all commotion going on in the lobby. There were pregnant girls, girls with babies, and men who were all in their own little world. One couple stuck out to me the most. The girl was about my age and she was watching while her baby's father fed their newborn son.

I got a little emotional thinking about my baby. That should've been me sitting there enjoying being a new mother. Instead, that opportunity was snatched away from me. I immediately tried to shake any negative thinking. I was trying to moved forward and forgive Miles for all his wrongdoings.

"Jhalani Givens!"

I gathered up my purse and headed to the back. The nurse greeted me and handed me a cup to go pee in. After I was finish, I sat in the room for a while waiting for the doctor to come in and do my exam. I was hoping that she'd hurry up because I was starving.

I heard a soft knock and then my doctor appeared in the doorway. She greeted me with a warm smile and asked me how I was doing.

"I'm great," I said.

She grabbed her stool and sat down looking over my chart, "Ms. Givens, are you aware that you're six weeks pregnant?"

What the fuck did she just say? I had to be in the fucking twilight zone.

I laughed, "Excuse me?"

"You're six weeks pregnant. You didn't know?" she asked staring at me over the top of her glasses.

"No, I didn't."

**

After leaving the doctor's office, I drove around for a few hours to clear my head. I didn't know what the fuck to do. Damien and I had messed around a few times unprotected but I thought I was good. I had quit my birth control a while back because of the irritating symptoms. I had even had my period so I assumed nothing was wrong. This news was totally unexpected and I was even more confused than I was before. How the hell do I tell Damien about a baby after what happened last night?

Tears streamed down my face as I pulled up in front of my house. I sat in the driveway with a million emotions flowing through me. I needed to talk to someone and the person I wanted to talk to was pissed at me. I wasn't sure if I wanted to tell Trinity because then I would have to tell her about Miles and I wasn't ready for that yet. Life sure knows how to throw you curve balls when you least expect it. I sat there with my phone in my hands debating on whether or not I should call her.

I pressed the telephone button and waited for her to answer.

"Hey boo," she answered on the second ring.

"Hey sis, are you busy?" I asked sniffling.

"No, what's wrong?"

"I need to talk. I'm about to come over," I said shifting my car in drive.

"Ok."

I backed out of the driveway and took the twenty-minute drive to her and Q's house. I took that time to get myself together so that I could deliver the news without crying. I also used that time to get my story together and leave out the part about Miles. I just wasn't ready to say anything about that just yet. I was even having second thoughts about meeting up with him later. Maybe I should just leave it alone.

When I pulled up in front of their house, I called her and asked if we could sit out back. I didn't want to be in the house because I wasn't sure if Q was home. I didn't need him to know just yet either. I needed time to process the information first. I know Dame was his right hand man and I didn't plan on telling him yet.

Trinity met me on the back patio with a glass of wine. When she handed it to me, unconsciously I gulped it down. I needed that more than anything right now. While I staring into space, Trinity was staring a hole into the side of my face.

"What's wrong sis? You're acting all weird and shit." Trinity said sipping from her glass.

"Trini, I'm pregnant again." I blurted out.

Her lips curled into a smile and jumped up to hug me. She didn't know that right now this was not a celebration. Before I knew it, I was in tears again. So much for not crying again huh? I wanted to share the same emotion Trinity was feeling at the moment. I just didn't know what to make of all this shit. Why did my life have to be so damn complicated?

"What's wrong boo?" Trinity asked when she noticed my tears staining her shirt.

"Everything. Damien and I got into it and he's mad at me right now. I haven't even told him yet," I said dabbing my eyes with a napkin.

"Aww boo, you guys will be fine. What did y'all get into it about?" she asked.

I shook my head, "I don't even want to talk about that right now."

"Well, you know I'm always here if you need me babe."

"I know sis. Please don't tell Q about this yet. I don't want Damien to find out just yet."

"I won't boo. You got my word," she paused, "Look sis, whatever is bothering you will work itself out ok? Don't stress yourself or my god-baby out over any nonsense."

"Thanks T. It's just so overwhelming. He won't even accept any calls from me. I don't know what the fuck to do." I said.

"He'll come around boo, you know that."

"I hope so. This shit is crazy."

I sat with Trinity and we talked until it got dark outside. She had me feeling a lot better than I did before I got here. This was one of the many reasons I loved Trinity. She always put me in a better headspace. She was real and uncut and sometimes I needed her rawness to help me see things clearer. Because of her I decided to try to contact Damien again and of course, no answer. It was all good though. I'd let him have his space. I'm sure he'll come around when he's ready.

QUARAN

I was sitting in my office going over the paperwork for two buildings I had just purchased. Shit had been smooth sailing over the last month as far as business goes. I was almost done setting up my legit businesses so that I could kiss this drug game goodbye. I didn't want to end up like my father, serving time for some bullshit. I wanted to get out while shit was good. Once I tied up a few loose ends, I was out. This shit was stressful as hell and I didn't want to deal with it anymore. Shit don't stay gravy forever and I needed out.

Ever since Trinity told me about the threats from her baby's father, I had been plotting on that too. I already knew it because Jade had already told Chevy. I didn't want Trinity to worry about shit. She already had enough shit going and I needed her to know that she was safe. I planned on talking to her about the situation and putting her up on game. I also needed to her to see how important it was for her to stop dancing. How the fuck she gone be safe at a well-known spot that everybody and their mama go to? She thought it was only because I didn't want her dancing, which was only part of the reason. Her safety was more important than anything to me. She was far from safe as long as the mothafuckas knew where she was working.

After I finished up my paperwork, I exited my office and made my way upstairs. Trinity and Gio were sprawled across the bed knocked out. I decided to hit the block for a minute and handle some more business. Scooter and Chevy had done a few pick-ups today and I needed to go collect my cash. Nothing made me happier than getting money, but I could honestly say I'd be even happier once I washed my hands of this drug game.

I got in my whip and sped toward the city. I called up Chevy and let him know that I was on my way and to have everybody there. Something was off about the last count and I hadn't mentioned it. I wanted everybody there so that if my shit was off this time, consequences would be handed out. Los had been MIA only coming through to pick up his weight. I had a feeling the nigga was being iffy. If my assumptions were right, he'd be a dead man before the night was out.

When I pulled up, everybody was in attendance except for Los. Disrespect was an all time around this bitch. Instead of these niggas being inside they were chopping shit up and kicking it on the porch. I shook my head as I walked the porch and right past them. All conversation seized and niggas followed me right in the basement of the crib. Everybody sat down and waited for me to start speaking.

"Where the fuck is Los?" I asked.

Scooter spoke up, "The nigga said he was on his way. I don't know where the fuck he is."

"Bet."

I sat at the head of the table and didn't say shit else until Los came staggering down the steps thirty minutes later. Dame, Chevy, and Scooter watched me as I watched him. It was obvious as hell this nigga was off his rocker. Looks like he's been using the product instead of selling it. See what I meant about everybody not being cut for this shit? I shook my head as he sat at the table buck eyed trying to look sober. He was high off his ass.

Rule number one was to never become a user. Never dab in your own product. Los was out here looking like one the fiends we see on a daily. This game wasn't for the weak. And right now, Los was proving how weak he was. I've stressed to these niggas on numerous occasions to never get hooked on this shit. This shit causes niggas to do crazy shit like steal from the nigga that was helping him provide for his family. Loyalty was most important to me and if a nigga couldn't give me loyalty, he couldn't give me shit.

"Wassup Los?" I asked with my hands crossed in front of me.

"Sh-shit, b-boss man. Wass good with you," he slurred and stuttered over his words.

"So, I called this quick meeting, one, to collect my money and also to pay you niggas," I said walking over to the five duffle bags in the corner.

I tossed one to Chevy, one to Scooter, and one to Dame. The other two I kept next to me. Los sat there confused as hell as to why he didn't get his duffy. He sat there looking back and forth between everybody wondering what was going on. These other niggas were confused as hell too. Didn't know what the fuck to expect.

"Los, you been using?" I asked pulling the pistol from my waistband and pointing it at Los' head.

His eyes bucked out of their socket, "N-n-nah man. I sw-swear to-to you."

I looked at him sideways, "I think you lying to me bro. Some of my product was missing last week and my money was short. You think I'm some goofy ass fuck nigga?" I asked pressing the pistol right in between his eyes.

"Nah Q, come on man," he said as tears streamed down his face.

Did he really think his pussy ass tears was gone stop me from putting this hot lead in his ass? I didn't give a fuck about his pleading. Didn't give a fuck about Scooter trying to talk me out of it. I didn't give a fuck about anything. I really didn't give a fuck when I squeezed the trigger and brain matter splattered everywhere. I tucked my gun back in my waist and sat back at the head of the table. Chevy and Damien sat there quietly and waited for me to speak. Scooter was in his feelings and I didn't care.

"Call the cleanup crew and dispose of this nigga," I said to Scooter.

He grabbed his phone and walked off.

"Damn bro. You on one today huh?" Dame asked relaxing in the chair.

"I ain't on shit. I've never tolerated disrespect, especially from a nigga in my circle." I said using a towel to wipe off my hands.

"I can't look at this shit no more, I'm out," Chevy said standing to his feet and tossing his duffle bag over his shoulder, "Catch y'all niggas later."

Damien watched as Chevy went upstairs and then asked, "Shits crazy. The nigga was stealing though? He wild as hell."

I shrugged, "Don't even matter anymore. The nigga's a memory now."

"So you still talking about leaving the game nigga?" Damien asked lighting a blunt and looking me in the eyes.

"Yeah nigga. I don't want this shit forever. I'm over straight on money. My time is up." I said leaning back and relaxing in the chair.

"So what you gone do with the business when you done?" he asked.

I shrugged. As of right now, that wasn't his business.

Dame had been real inquisitive about my leaving the game. Lately it was all he talked about. I knew Dame was eager to run shit but he wouldn't be doing so without my permission. Niggas thought this shit was easy. It wasn't. Every decision you make affects you and the people around you. There is no room for fuck ups in this business. Murking off Los wasn't something I wanted to do but I had to do it.

I shook my head as the cleanup crew carried his body up the stairs and out the back door. I didn't have room for any snakes in my circle. My shit had always been ran tight and it will continue to be that way. Whatever his reason for using and stealing from me must have been important enough for him to die over. Niggas don't think before they start making irrational decisions. When you only living for the moment, you don't think smart. But oh well, niggas die every day.

**

"What's wrong baby?" Trinity asked wrapping her arms around me while I stood in the mirror looking at my reflection.

"I'm good shorty," I said taking my chain off my neck.

"You sure? You look stressed," she said running her hands up and down my back.

"Positive," I said laying across our California king bed.

Trinity climbed on my back and sat down. She pulled my wife beater over my head and began to slowly massage my back. I looked at her reflection in the mirror and admired how beautiful she was. We had been vibing like crazy lately. Her soft hands felt like silk against my skin. She massaged my back like a professional and I instantly relaxed. This is exactly what I needed after the stressful day I had. Lil mama had a nigga on a cloud.

"It looks like you stressing out to me baby," Trinity said massaging my arms.

"Look shorty, whatever happens out there in the streets is between me and the streets. I don't want you worried about shit that goes on out there. Just know that I'm good when you around."

"Alright, I'm sorry. You're right. I just don't like seeing you like that."

I looked at her through the mirror, "I'm good shorty, always will be."

She leaned down and kissed the back of my neck.

She was on a tip tonight. I knew it when I felt her soft lips tracing up my spine. I groaned a little when she licked my earlobe. I turned over and placed her on my dick. I massaged her thighs as she stared at me with lust in her eyes. I grabbed her shirt, pulled her down to me and kissed her. I separated her lips with my tongue and sucked on her full bottom lip. She moaned into my mouth when my hands found her nipples through the thin fabric of her shirt. I traced my kisses down the side of her face and to her neck where I lingered for a little bit.

"I love you Quaran."

"I love you too Trinity."

I lifted her over me until her pussy was right in my face. I pulled her lace panties to the side and dipped my tongue into her wetness. She tasted good as fuck. Sweet, like all she ate was fruits. Her breathing became labored as stiffened my tongue and rocked it back and forth over her sensitive clit. She moaned and threw her head back as bounced on my tongue like she was riding my dick. I gripped her ass cheeks tightly to keep her from falling.

After she released, I sucked up every bit of her. She climbed off of me and hungrily grabbed for my belt buckle. She helped me pulled down my jeans and boxers and tossed them to the floor. She stared at my hard dick with lust, licking her lips as she admired it. She eased down and wrapped her wet mouth around me while she stroked softly. I threw my head back enjoying the feeling of her tongue swirling around the head of my dick. Trinity was a beast when it came to giving head. Shorty should definitely be giving out classes or some shit. It was like she took her time to perfect what she was doing.

The more she sucked, the wetter her mouth got. There was so much spit and the way she was stroking me I was bound to cum any minute. I looked down and she was watching me. She eased my dick down her throat slowly, never breaking the eye contact. She was sexy as fuck and I had to look away before I bust all down her throat. I could feel my nut rising as she used both hands to stroke me and suck on the tip of my dick. I pulled her up and sat her on my dick. Her mouth made an O shape as she adjusted to me entering her. I groaned enjoying the feeling of sliding into her. Her pussy was the tightest, wettest, warmest I had ever been in. She began to slowly bounce up and down as she got used to my size.

I spread her ass cheeks and slammed her down onto my dick. She yelled out and kept bouncing. I did it again and again she screamed out.

"Be quiet before you wake up Gio," I told her kissing her as she moaned.

"I'm sorry daddy," she said slowing up her pace.

I pulled her off of me and patted her on the ass, "Turn over."

She laid down on her stomach and tooted her perfectly round ass up in the air. I smacked it and then placed a kiss on her each of her ass cheeks. I spread them again and watched as I eased my dick into her wetness again. She moaned into the bed as she gripped the sheets. Her arch was perfect. I knew from the way she was bucking against me that I wouldn't last long. I pulled out and slammed back into her, slapping her ass again.

"Mm, baby you feel so good inside of me." she said.

I licked my thumb and ran it up and down the crack of her ass. She moaned again. I slipped my thumb right in her ass and she moaned even louder. Trinity was a straight up freak. As I slammed my dick in and out of her, I slipped my thumb in and out of her ass. She was enjoying every minute of it.

"You like that shit?" I asked.

She whimpered, "Yes. I'm about to cum."

I picked up my pace and slammed into her middle. I was on the verge of a nut too. Shorty slipped her hand in between her legs and massaged her clit. Got damn. I loved watching her play with herself. When her muscles began clenching around my dick, I knew she was about to cum. I took my thumb out her ass and spread her ass cheeks so I could go deeper.

"Shit baby. You got some good ass pussy," I said watching as my dick became heavily coated with her cum.

"Q, don't bust inside me."

It was too good to pull out. I couldn't help it. I released right inside her sweet ass walls and collapsed on top of her.

"You so fucking hard headed," she said breathlessly.

It is what it is. That pussy was too good to pull out of. She was just being noid. It ain't like I nut in her all the time. This was only the first time we've fucked without a condom. If she didn't want me cumming inside her, we were definitely going to have to stick to the condoms. Her pussy had a nigga pull out game weak as hell.

TRINITY

When I woke up the next morning, Q was gone. I stretched and lazily climbed out of bed. My body was sore as shit from the beating Q had put on me last night. I pulled the curtains in our room back and went straight to the bathroom. I walked over to the, his and hers sinks and grabbed my toothbrush and the toothpaste. I smiled to myself as I replayed last night events. I needed that good sex. I was so happy that Gio knocked out early last night. He's usually in our room and by the time he does fall asleep, I'm usually asleep with him. It felt good to connect with my man last night. Q and I had been on a cloud these past few weeks.

He was doing good with starting up his businesses and trying to get out the game. I know it wasn't easy for him because he's done it for so long. To see him trying to become a better man and make better decisions, had me in feelings. Not in a bad way though. I loved how much he strives to become better. I was happy as hell because being in line of work was dangerous as hell. Even though he constantly stressed to me not to worry, I couldn't do anything but worry. Quaran was a big part of my life now and I don't know what I would do if something ever happened to him. Safety wasn't always guaranteed and I needed him to come home to me every night.

Last night was one of those rare nights we got to spend some alone time. Usually, were out kicking it or we were busy entertaining Gio. I enjoyed every minute of last night. I looked at my reflection and smiled at myself. I had a glow that said I was in a happy space. I always wondered how women got that glow, but I know now. I had been enjoying every minute of the happy space I was in.

The other night when Jade delivered the news about Geno to me, I instantly went into a funk. Wondering why this nigga was trying so hard to bring me down. For as I long as I had known him, he's never been this conniving. His bitterness toward me was controlling his every move now. What type of nigga sits up and plots on his child's mother? He had always hated how independent I was. The fact that I have never needed him for anything had always bothered him. I always made sure Gio was good, with or without his ass.

The fact that Q had come in and swooped me off my feet and was now helping me take care of Gio, annoyed the fuck out of Geno. It was funny to me how he didn't want to do anything as far as taking care of Gio. Only when it was convenient for him. Now he has the nerve to have a whole other baby out here. He was pathetic. When Q told me not to worry about shit and that he would handle it, my cares went out the window. Geno had never put fear in me and he wouldn't start now. Whatever him and his baby's mother were planning weren't going to stop me from living. I had always been careful and I just made sure to be extra careful now. Geno was no match for Q and if my man said don't worry about it, then I wouldn't.

"Ma, can you make some pancakes?"

I looked up and Gio was standing in my doorway with his iPad.

I shook my head, "Yeah son, give me a minute."

I took a quick shower and threw on a jogging suit. I headed downstairs to prepare breakfast for Gio when my phone began ringing. It was my mother.

"Hey ma," I said as I grabbed the griddle from underneath the cabinet.

"Hey Trini, open up the door. I'm outside." She said.

I sat the griddle down and made my way to the living room. I had missed my mama since I hadn't seen much of her lately. Her and my daddy had been vacationing living the life. I couldn't wait until I was able to do that.

I opened up the door and greeted her with a hug. My mama was looking fine as wine. Looking like she was my age. She followed me to the kitchen and sat her bag on the table while she hugged Gio. My baby was crazy about his Nanny.

"So what have you been up to little girl?" she asked sitting at the island.

I stirred the pancake mix and looked at her, "Nothing, work and here with Gio. Same old routine."

"Oh ok. I went to the casino the other night with Rita. We stopped by to say hi and I asked one of the mangers if you were there."

My heart began to beat out of my chest, "Oh really? What day?"

She crossed her arms across her chest and looked at me, "Well see, it doesn't really matter what day because they told they didn't have an employee named Trinity."

I laughed nervously, "They must have been playing with you ma."

She gave me a stern look, "Trinity Marie Hayes, stop playing with me. Have you been lying to me all these years about working at that damn casino?"

I sighed and looked away. I knew this moment would come sooner or later. I just wished it wasn't right now. I was stuck not knowing what to say. I was afraid of what she would think of me. Would she judge me? Hell, would she disown me? I didn't know and the unknown had me shook. I stood there unmoving while she stared me down.

I took a deep breath and sighed, "Yes."

She threw her hands up, "Ok...So exactly where the hell have you been working? Don't lie to me either."

"The Pink Lounge," I said holding my breath.

Her eyes grew big, "So what are you? A waitress or a bartender?"

I looked away and stared the wall. My palms were sweaty as hell and my heartbeat had to be at a thousand beats per minute.

I looked her right in the eye and said, "No, I dance there."

Her mouth dropped. In that moment, I regretted telling her. I felt like I had made the biggest mistake in my life. Her eyes welled up with tears as she looked at me. My heart broke. The look in her eyes as she stared me hurt me to the core. I never wanted her to find out but I couldn't keep lying to her. I had been keeping this secret for far too long. As much as it hurt to say it out loud to her, I felt good to have the weight lifted off my shoulders.

"Why Trini?" she asked lowly.

I took a deep breath and looked her in the eyes again, "When you and daddy put me out when I got pregnant, I didn't know what else to do. Y'all put me in an apartment, paid the rent for two months and told me to make it work. I didn't know anything about working. I swear to you, I started off bartending. It was cool at first until I saw how much money those other girls were racking in. So, I tried it. I became addicted to the fast money and I've been dancing ever since."

She remained quiet so I kept talking.

"Mama, I know you may be disappointed, disgusted even. I never wanted to hurt you or daddy in any way. I just didn't want to be a failure, out here struggling trying to take care of my baby. I'm sorry."

After a few minutes of silence, she finally spoke.

"I'm not disgusted Trinity, just disappointed. I would never cast judgement on you baby girl but there were other options. I'm more pissed off that you have been lying to me and your father all these years."

"Ma, I didn't want to but I didn't know how to tell y'all. As you can see this isn't an easy conversation to have." I said, "Are you going to tell Daddy?"

She looked at me and sighed, "No, I'll keep this between me and you," she paused, "Only if you quit."

I rolled my eyes. Everybody was trying to get me to quit. I didn't oppose the idea but I needed to secure another source of income. I could not and would not sit around and allow Q to take care of me. That wasn't who I was. I needed to be doing something. While the idea of not getting that fast money scared me, I had to woman up someday. I knew that dancing wouldn't last forever. I pondered on the idea and realized quitting would be best. The idea of my father finding out about me dancing sickened me. I couldn't taint the image of me that my father had. She stood up and pulled me into her arms. I shed a few tears as we stood there holding each other.

"Alright ma, I'll quit."

**

"You told your fucking mother?! Wow," Jhalani said as we ate burrito bowls at Chipotle.

I nodded my head up and down as I stuffed my face. I needed someone to vent to. Q was handling business and my mother had taken Gio to Toys R Us. I couldn't sit home alone with my thoughts. They would drive me crazy. I sat around all day praying that my mother wouldn't slip and tell my father about me. She was usually good at keeping secrets but I felt like this one was too juicy not to tell. I had been feeling some type of way since she had left my house earlier.

"Damn sis, you're brave as hell. What did she say? Oh my gawd, I can't believe you told," Jhalani said being dramatic as hell.

"You're so extra right now," I laughed.

"Bitch, this is big news."

I waved her off, "She cried, then she hugged me and told me I had to quit."

"So what are you gonna do? You've been saying you wanted to quit anyway," She said wiping her mouth with a napkin.

I shrugged, "I have no idea. I want to quit, just not now. I need to stack up just a little more."

Jhalani rolled her eyes, "Cut it out bitch. You know just like I do, your savings is beyond good."

I laughed and pointed my fork at her, "You are one nosey bitch, you know that?"

She shrugged, "And?"

We laughed together and shared small talk while we ate. I wanted to ask her how she had been doing with her pregnancy but it might I have been a touchy subject. She hadn't mentioned it since she first told me and I didn't want to press her to talk about it. She seemed to be doing okay and that was enough for me.

The dinging of the door caused me to draw my attention to the front. Especially when Jhalani's eyes locked in on something behind me. I turned around to see Miles and some chick walking hand in hand into the restaurant. I was stunned because the last time I had seen him he looked terrible. Here he was though, standing in Chipotle with another woman looking fresh as hell. I pulled my attention away from them and looked at Jhalani. She had a perplexed look on her face.

"You see that shit?" she finally said.

I nodded and asked her if she was ok.

"He's coming over here," she said dropping her fork.

When I turned around, sure enough he was heading for our table. I looked at Jhalani and she was antsy as hell. Miles walked up to the table with his hands up, I guess as his peace offering. I rolled my eyes. I couldn't stand his sorry ass. The fact that he was standing beside our table annoyed the fuck out of me. I turned around and continued eating my food. He spoke to me but I ignored him.

Jhalani placed her hands under her chin and stared at Miles as he introduced her to his girlfriend. Jhalani rolled her eyes and excused herself from the table. I was confused as hell right now. I didn't know what the fuck was going on with Jhalani lately. She had been acting strange since she told me she was pregnant. Something was up and If I didn't know any better, I would swear she was feeling some type of way right now about seeing Miles. The way she acted at the mention of his name a few months ago was crazy. Today it's as if she's been around him recently.

I went into the bathroom and I could hear her throwing up in one of the stalls.

"Sis, you okay?" I asked.

She yelled over the flushing of the toilet, "Yeah."

She came out of the stall smoothing her shirt over her joggers. Her eyes were puffy and red. She looked at me and then at herself in the mirror.

"What's wrong Lani?"

"I'm still in love with Miles," she said dropping her head.

I instantly became pissed, "What you mean you still in love with Miles?"

"I don't know. I'm confused as shit right now. I don't know why these feelings came back. I've been trying to get rid of them for a while. Ever since I met up with Sasha about him and she's told me how good he's doing, I can't stop thinking about him."

I shook my head, "Jhalani please. That nigga damn near beat you to death. That should have taken all your feelings away."

She huffed, "I should have known you wouldn't understand. You never fucking do."

"Excuse me?" I said with my eyebrow raised, "I'm sorry I care so much about my best friend that I'm not open to listening to her talk about how she's still in love with a nigga that almost killed her."

"But let me deal with that. That was then Trini, he's changed. You see how well he looks? That should be me prancing around with him all happy and shit."

"Oh Jhalani please. You gotta be fucking with me right now, right? I know you ain't serious," I said laughing.

She didn't though. She was dead ass serious.

"I'm leaving Trinity. I'll talk you later," She said and rushed out of the door.

I was confused as hell right now. What the fuck did I do? Was she really mad at me for caring about her? I know she didn't think for one minute that I would be ok with that shit. Jhalani was tripping hard as hell. I exited the bathroom and saw her car pulling out of the parking lot. I called her phone and she sent me to voicemail. I called her two more times and nothing. I let out an exasperated breath and threw my phone into my purse. If she wanted to act like an ass then fuck it.

**

Jhalani must have been really pissed off at me because even after four hours, she still hadn't answered or returned my calls. I was annoyed as hell but what could I do? I couldn't force her to talk to me. I wasn't going to try either. She was being a bitch all because I care about her. I wished she cared about herself enough to realize that she shouldn't be dealing with a nigga like Miles. She was being so stupid and she should understand where I was coming from.

"Trinity, calm down. She'll come around. Her hormones going crazy right now." Candice said watching me pace around.

"I can't believe she's acting like this though Sug."

Jhalani didn't even show up for work tonight. Moonie told us she called him and said she needed a few days off. When I showed up tonight, I was expecting to talk to her and sort out our differences. I wanted to apologize for making her feel however she was feeling but she wasn't trying to hear shit I was saying. I let it go. If she wanted to talk, she had my number.

I gulped down my water and headed to the floor with Candice in tow. Money still had to be made. Q's birthday was coming up in a few short weeks and I was trying to throw him a surprise party. I needed every last dollar to make sure it was a success. After I built up my coins, I'd quit. I hadn't told Moonie I planned on quitting yet. He'd be upset about losing his best girl but I know he would support my decision. He never really wanted me dancing anyway.

When I got out front, I spotted Moonie talking to Geno. I scrunched up my face and elbowed Candice. When she saw what I was looking at, she became confused.

"The fuck is he doing here?" she asked.

"I have no idea. I'll find out in a minute."

I walked around and gave a few dances, making sure to keep my eyes on them. It looked like whatever they were talking about was a mellow conversation. They must have been discussing some type of business. When Geno walked away and out of the club, I gathered up my money and walked over to Moonie.

"Bro, what the fuck was he doing up here?"

Moonie looked at me over his shoulder, "Trying to get Strawberry her job back. Gave me some bread to let her come back to work. I told his ass next time she go MIA, she ain't gotta worry about coming back."

"Ugh, that bitch coming back?"

He looked over his shoulder, "Yea. Behave T. I don't want any altercations. She's getting ready now."

I rolled my eyes and walked off. Moonie didn't really know anything about my situation with them. Only thing he knew is that Strawberry and I had some petty ass girl beef. I kept private about it with Moonie because he doesn't want any drama up here. He wouldn't hesitate to fire my ass right along with her if he got wind of the bullshit. I decided to keep quiet and let shit play out.

I got right back to work as I spotted one of my usual customers heading toward me. He was cool guy. He had a bag and he always came to support me on the weekends. He'd even bring his girl with him sometimes and they'd cash out on me. He grabbed my hand and led to an empty table in the back of the club. He sat down and I immediately started dancing for him. Speaker Knockerz came through the speakers and I went crazy.

I'ma throw this money like a free throw
You just keep on dancing, like a freak ho
Arch your back, put your hands on your knees ho
Bounce that ass to my muthafuckin beat ho
Bounce that ass, bounce that ass
Bounce that ass, bounce that ass

I had my hands on my knees, twerking my ass to the beat. I looked back and bent down and jiggled my ass on the crotch of his jeans. The singles were raining down on me as was working my ass off literally.

After the song ended, I headed to find Sugar. I was headed to the VIP area when I felt someone bump the shit out of me, almost knocking me over. When I regained my composure, I looked up and saw the back of Strawberry's head. I walked up behind her and shoved the shit out of her. She spun around and tried to swing on me. Her fist skinned my cheek, barely missing it. I swung with everything I had in me, landing a blow right to the side of her head.

After scuffling for a few more seconds, I felt myself being lifted off the ground. Security was grabbing up both of our asses. I was so mad; I was trying to fight them off of me. I spotted Moonie coming toward us with a scowl on his face. I know he was pissed especially after he had just told me to behave. It wasn't my fault though.

"T, what the fuck I just tell y'all?" he yelled.

"That was this raggedy ass bitch!" I yelled back pointing at Strawberry.

"Both of y'all gotta go."

I pushed security off of me and headed toward the back. Fuck Moonie, fuck this club, and fuck these hating ass bitches. I never bother any fucking body but everybody wants to fuck with me. I came to work to make my money, nothing else. It was cool doe, I had more than enough cash to throw Q's party. I was tired; tired of all the drama, tired of this damn club, and tired of trying to hold myself together. I was fuming as I slammed all of my things into my PINK bag. I was going to wait to quit but fuck it, better now than later.

I understood Moonie's stance on making me leave. I understood he had a business to run but he knows me and he knows I'm far from a troublemaker. For a while Strawberry and Jade were a problem for me and he knew that. Still, he allowed them bitches to continue to work here. For so long, I ignored their ugly stares and childish antics for the sake of being professional at work. Moonie knew all that too, so fuck him and The Pink Lounge.

As I was grabbing the last of my things, Sugar came to the back and watched me pack. She wore a mug on her face too. I saw her trying to get to me but security wouldn't let her.

"You leaving boo?" she asked.

"For good."

She gasped, "Damn boo, who the fuck I'ma cut up in here with now?"

"I don't know Sug, but I gotta go. I cannot do this anymore."

We talked for a few minutes and I told her I would hit her up later. I left out the back and saw Strawberry still being held up in a corner by security. I mouthed 'bitch' to her as I walked past. Moonie was standing by the bar, gawking at me. I flipped him the bird and walked out for the last time. I tossed my bag over my shoulder and walked to my car. The lot was fairly empty and there were a few people scattered about. I hit the locks on my truck and tossed my bag in the back seat.

When I stepped back to close the door, I felt someone wrap their arm around my neck. I clawed at the arm as I struggled to breath, when I noticed the familiar 'G' tattoo on his hand. It was Geno. Fear paralyzed me and I struggled to stay awake. Life felt like it was leaving my body. I felt like I was in the twilight zone. I prayed like fuck I wouldn't be taken out by this pussy ass nigga. Why the fuck was shit constantly happening to me? I couldn't catch a break for shit. It was one thing after the other.

"Bitch, you thought you was untouchable huh?" he said through gritted teeth. He released his grip on my neck and grabbed a handful of my hair.

I choked trying to catch my breath. I was gasping for air as he yanked my head around.

"You riding around acting like you better than me bitch. Talking shit to my baby mama like you don't need me, like I ain't shit. Fuck you Trinity, you and your son. I don't need either one of y'all. I got me a new family since you went and got you one," he said yanking my head up to look at him, "Got that pussy ass nigga Q riding around with you and my son like he the fucking man. Got my son all around that nigga like he birthed him. Fuck is wrong with you?"

I was still gasping for air, "Fu-fuck you, Gen-Geno."

He pulled my hair again and slapped me in the face, "Bitch, I will fucking kill you out here."

I didn't give a fuck. If I was about to die, I was going to talk shit anyway, fuck Geno. "You ain't, ain't shit, never have been. Ole has been ass ni-nigga," I said elbowing him in his stomach.

He grabbed his stomach, "Bitch!"

SKURRR!

My fucking savior. Quaran. I watched his Audi speed down the block toward the club. Geno's attention shifted to the commotion coming toward us. I elbowed him again and he let my hair go, finally. Geno panicked and hopped in his old school and sped off. A few seconds later, Q was pulling up behind me. He hopped out his truck, barely putting it in park. I ran over to him and broke down in his arms. He squeezed me so tight that I instantly felt safe.

"Fuck!" he yelled.

I have no clue how the hell he knew what was going on but I was thankful. Shit could have gotten real ugly for me. I was pissed that Geno got away before Q got here. Quaran was looking like a fucking mad man. The look Quaran wore on his face told me shit was about to get ugly. He held me and called up his boys. While he talked, he put me in his car and stood outside of his truck giving orders.

"I want that mothafucka dead tonight!"

QUARAN

Bloodshed. That's the only thing I could think about right now. The only thing that was on my mental was making blood rain all over the streets of Chicago. I can't believe this hoe ass nigga thought it was cool to put hands on shorty. Straight up fucking pussy. Pulling shorty hair, choking her, that was some bitch ass shit. What type of nigga does that to a woman? A fuck nigga. I'm mad as fuck that shit went down like that and I wasn't there to protect my shorty. This clown can roll up on her but won't pull up on me.

Once me and shorty made it to the crib, I had her call her girls to come sit with her. I needed to hit the streets and rid them of low life ass niggas. Once Candice arrived, I dipped. I called up my niggas and met up with them. I was riding through the low end with my niggas looking for pussy boy. I had the K tucked on the side of my seat and I was itching to use that bitch. We pulled up to the crib where Dame let off the shots the last time. I parked a few cribs down and watched for any activity. Only car in front of the house was a black Charger.

I sat quietly thinking and calculating. I'm almost sure the nigga wasn't dumb enough to come back here. By now he knows I'm looking for his ass. I'm sure there's someone in this bitch that could be useful. When I saw a shadowy figure move up the porch, I told Dame, Chevy, and Scooter to mask up. I hopped out of the truck in all back with the K at my side. Dame was on the side of me with the chopper. Chevy and Scooter had my back.

Dame and I went to the back and Chevy and Scooter watched the front door. I carefully walked on the side of the house, careful not to make noise. I heard two niggas talking in the back. I looked back at Dame and pointed to my leg, telling him to cripple the niggas and not to kill them. Not yet anyway. I nodded and Dame went ahead of me. He lifted the gun and walked in the back, disturbing the conversation.

"Don't fucking move!" said Dame aiming his gun at the two young niggas.

"Boy-boy, hand off your waistband. Toss that mothafucka right here," I said aiming the K at head.

"Fuck," he mumbled tossing the pistol at my feet.

"Where the fuck is Geno," Dame asked the shorter of the two.

"Geno ain't been here all day, we don't know shit." he said.

Dame was grilling the fuck out of dude, "What's yo name nigga? Don't lie either."

"Man, fuck y'all niggas," he said.

Dame let off in his leg, shattering it instantly. Tough guy fell to the ground, screaming in agony. Dame had the gun in his chest. I still had my gun aimed on the taller one. He had fear in his eyes. His jaw clenched as he watched the shorter feel for his limb.

I nodded at him, "What's your homies name?"

"Jody! What the fuck is all that noi-

I looked up and Strawberry was coming out the back door of the house. When she saw Dame and I standing there with the gun on who I assumed was Jody, she stopped in her tracks. She quickly turned on her heels and tried to run. It was too late though, Chevy had her ass hemmed up by her shirt with the burner in her back. Her tears instantly covered her face as she began begging for her life. I didn't give one fuck though.

"Bitch shut the fuck up." Chevy said.

I looked down at Jody with the K pointed in his face, "What's your relationship to her?"

He began shaking as he tried to speak, "My girl."

I thought back to when Trinity repeatedly told me about that black Charger that was always around when shit was going down with them. It was there at the robbery, and it was there at scuffle at the mall. It dawned on me, this was the nigga that robbed them. I eyed him as he struggled with his injury.

"Can y'all let me go?" said the taller one, "I ain't have shit to do with this. I only came over here for some weed."

"No witnesses," Dame said and sent a shot into his head. His body went limp and he collapsed to the ground, face to face to with Jody. He began struggling trying to move away. Strawberry's gut wrenching screams were annoying the fuck out of me. Bitch was sitting here crying like she wasn't guilty of shit. I usually didn't do hits on women but fuck it. Before I had the chance, Chevy sent a shot right into the back of her head.

Jody squirmed as his girl's brain matter splashed everywhere, "Ahh, fuck! Y'all ain't have to do that to her."

"Y'all ain't have to do a lot of the shit y'all did. Now I'ma ask you one last time, where is Geno nigga?"

"I told you man, ahhh," he yelled in agony, "I don't know. He ain't been around here in a few da-

BLAH!

I let the K rip his face off.

We walked from the back and casually walked to the truck. I could hear sirens in the distance. We hopped in the truck and I drove off just as five bent the corner. I had to find Geno soon.

**

When we walked in the crib, I was still in deep thought. I was riding through his mother in law's crib tomorrow. The bloodshed was far from over. I was mad as fuck his bitch ass wasn't there. I figured he wouldn't be but it still annoyed me that he was still running the streets. Chevy, Dame, and Scooter were sitting around the table talking shit. I wasn't listening though. My mind was on other shit. I had to take care of this nigga pronto. Wasn't no way I was sleeping unless this nigga was sleeping permanently. All I could think about was him putting his hands on my girl. Every time the thought crossed my mind, I cringed.

"You good Q?" Chevy asked.

I nodded and kept staring at the off white wall across the room.

"You looked stressed as hell, my nigga," Chevy said passing me the blunt he lit.

I took it from him and took a long pull from it. The smoke filled my lungs as I sat back and closed my eyes. Exhaling, I thought about all the shit that had been going on. I was tired of it. Too much was going on and I wasn't doing a good job of handling it. I felt like a clown for not being there for her when she needed me. Shit was eating at me like crazy. All I could think about is all the shit that she had been going through over the last few months. This nigga out here disrespecting the fuck out of her over some envious shit. Once this nigga was dead, I was done with this shit.

"Brodie, you straight fool?" Dame asked looking at me.

"I'm good. I'm just ready to put this nigga in the dirt. This pussy out here disrespecting in the worst way."

"I feel you bro, we'll find his ass." He said.

"It's been too damn long. I'm ready to off this nigga and be done with this shit." I said pulling from the blunt again.

Dame nodded, "You right. You still leaving the game?"

I looked at him again as I pulled from the blunt. What the fuck was this nigga's obsession with me leaving the game? He had been acting iffy as shit lately. Always questioning me leaving the game. Dame was my nigga but if need be, he'd catch a bullet too. Something has been different ever since he shot Trinity. I couldn't put my finger on it though. He was still looking at me awaiting an answer. He never got it. I ignored his ass and kept smoking.

When I finished, I got up grabbed my shit and left. Once I made it to the car, I pulled my phone out my back pocket and called Chevy. He answered on the first ring.

"Yo?" he answered.

"Aye, keep an eye on Dame. Nigga been iffy." I said.

He said, "Bet."

I hung up the phone and sped to the crib. I missed shorty and all I wanted to do right now was feel her body against mine. I made a promise to myself that this would be the last time he would be able to cause harm to her. Shorty ain't have to live, looking over shoulder all the time. She didn't deserve that shit.

I pulled up to the crib and Candice's car was still outside. The sun was about to come up soon and I was dead ass tired. I was praying shorty was in a guest room or some shit. When I unlocked the door, Trinity was sitting on the couch blankly staring at the TV. She looked over at me and smiled. Her hair was disheveled and her eyes were puffy as hell. I walked over to the couch and sat down next to her. She put down the remote and climbed in my lap.

"I was worried about you, I couldn't sleep."

"You ain't ever gotta worry about me shorty, I told you that. If ever I'm out in the streets on dirt, be worried for them," I said wrapping my arms around her.

"You find 'em?" she asked looking up at me.

"Not yet," I said, "Look, I need to you quit now ma, it ain't sa-

"I quit already," she said burying her face in my chest.

I didn't say anything else. I just held her and thought about what she said. That alone took weight off me. I didn't have to worry about her being up there anymore. I'm sure she would visit from time to time but at least she wouldn't be working there. I was about to ask her something else until I heard her lightly snoring. I grabbed the blanket had on the couch and wrapped it around her and passed out myself.

**

The next morning, I made sure Trinity was straight before I hit the block again. I was getting ready to meet with Chevy. I didn't even bother calling Dame. I needed to be investigating his ass to. There were always snakes in the game and even your closest homie couldn't be trusted. I never thought I would have to question Damien's loyalty but people and things change. The thing with this top spot is that you could look out for everybody the same, take care of 'em, and even put 'em on. For some niggas it would still never be enough. Mothafuckas sit back and watch your every move with envy, wishing they had that spot.

I didn't want to think this was my man's but he was showing all the traits of a fuck nigga. Always questioning whether or not I was leaving the game like he wanted my spot. I gave Damien the passenger seat to this shit but he was acting like he wanted to be the driver. He was eating good off me, why wasn't it enough? I always looked out and he was able to call shots when I wasn't available. He had major pull out here because of me. Niggas respected Dame because he put the work in for me. I could have left my homie out here bad when his people died, instead I looked out. So why was this nigga trying me? Whenever I left the game, of course I would hand it to Dame. But this nigga was acting like he was trying to push me out the way.

I told Chevy to watch him because right now, he was the only nigga proving his loyalty. Scooter's punk ass had been in his feelings since Los got his shit blew back. Acting like a bitch over a disloyal nigga. This is what I meant when I say most niggas ain't cut out for this shit. You gotta have the heart for this shit. You can't be out here in your feelings over shit you can't control.

When I pulled in front of Chevy's crib, he was already outside. He peeped me and jogged up to the car. He hopped in and dapped me up.

"What's good nigga?" he asked.

"Shit. Need to bend a few blocks and see if I spot this nigga."

"Let's go." Chevy said. He reclined the seat and pulled his black hood over his head.

In the street, yeah yeah
In the street, yeah yeah
I done shed blood in the street, yeah yeah
I done lost my blood in the street, yeah yeah
I done sold a lotta drugs in the street, yeah yeah
In the street, yeah yeah
M.O.B, yeah yeah
I done ran it up in the street, yeah yeah
I got set up in the street, yeah yeah
I done fell in love with the street, yeah yeah

Lucci's Bloodshed played through the speakers as we rode through the city. I was riding through the all the known spots around the hood trying to see if he was out. Where the fuck does this nigga hide out at? He's never anywhere most hood niggas hung out. I was convinced he was just some goofy ass nigga out here trying to get some clout.

Chevy leaned up his seat, "Aye there go that bitch Jade walking in the gas station."

I made a left turn and stopped in front of her. She looked up like she'd seen a ghost. Her body relaxed when she realized it was Chevy in the car.

"Get in." he told her as I popped the locks.

She hesitantly climbed in the back seat. I pulled off soon she closed the door. It was silent as I drove her to a quiet block. Once we were in front of the park, I put the car in park and killed the engine.

"What's up with this nigga Geno?" I asked her looking at her in the rearview mirror.

She looked away, "If you're asking if I know where he is, I don't know."

"Why the fuck can't I ever find his ass?"

She shrugged, "I don't know. He's never told us where he goes. All I really know is that he was gunning for you over some petty shit."

"Why?" I asked.

She sighed, "He had always been watching you. He was obsessed with you way before Trinity came into the picture. He used to talk about getting close to you so that you could put him back on. When he saw you that day with Trinity, he became overly obsessed. He thought through her he could get close to you. Aint no real beef, the nigga is just a fucking jealous ass clown. He ain't never really expect for this shit to spiral out of control like this."

"So you have no clue where the nigga could be?" Chevy asked turning around to face her.

"Not one. I'm trying to get the fuck out of here. I didn't want shit to do with any of this. I got drug into this shit by Strawberry. He got her sister brainwashed and he's been threatening me ever since I called you about him attacking Trinity." She said nervously looking around, "Could you take me back to the gas station. I need to get some shit before I leave."

"One last thing, his baby mom's still staying at that crib we saw you at?"

"Yea."

"Aight."

I dropped shorty off back at the gas station and headed in the direction of the crib she told us about. Apart of me felt bad for her. Caught up in some shit she wanted no parts of. It's a shame what jealousy could do to a person. Got this clown dragging people into shit they didn't have anything to do with.

I was about to post up at this nigga's people crib and wait. He was bound to show up sooner or later.

JHALANI

I had been keeping to myself lately. That day I saw Miles with that girl sent me over the edge. How could he lead me on like he wanted me then flaunt some chick in my face like it was cool? I had long ago stopped trying to fight what I was feeling. I know you think I'm crazy and I probably am. If we didn't work out this time, then I'd let it go. We had been texting and seeing a lot more of each other since the Chipotle incident. We were in a much better space than ever before.

I still hadn't told Damien about my pregnancy. I was afraid to. What if he wasn't happy about it? What would I do? He was still pissed off at me for the way our date ended that night. I couldn't blame him. I felt like shit for the way shit went down. I never wanted shit to go like that between us. Damien had been there for me whenever I needed and I do some shit like this to him. He expressed his anger through a text he sent me a few days ago saying he would contact me when he was ready. My feelings were slightly hurt but what could I do? If I was him, I would have probably reacted the same way.

I had even texted Trinity to apologize to her but she was also mad at me. She texted to check on me here and there but we hadn't hung out or anything since then. I know I overreacted to her not agreeing with my relationship with Miles but I just wanted someone to see things my way. I've come to terms with the fact that no one will be accepting of me trying to work things out with him. Trinity was my best friend and I just wanted her support on my decision. I had to remember that she wasn't that friend to just go along with shit she didn't agree with. Again, I have to do this for me. Back in the day, this was all I ever wanted.

Currently, I was lying in bed thinking about the date I went on with Miles last night. He was so different than the last time we had been together. I wasn't 'bitch' anymore; I was baby or just plain Lani now. It felt good to get the attention I had been yearning for from him. He was so sweet and attentive just like he had been before he spiraled out of control. We went to eat a nice bar and grill downtown on the lakefront. I actually enjoyed myself.

I rolled over on my side, seeing that I had a text notification.

Miles (9:47AM): *Good morning beautiful.*

I texted him back and got up to grab something to eat. This baby had been kicking my ass. I was hungry more frequently and sleeping so much. Nobody knew about my pregnancy except for Trinity and Candice. I hadn't told my parents yet because I was waiting to tell Damien first. I needed to tell him pronto because I was almost three months along. My biggest fear was rejection from him for our baby. I didn't take him as that type but the way he was feeling about me now, I couldn't tell.

After feeding my belly, I got dressed. I had decided to drive over to Damien's in a little bit to try and talk to him. I had a movie date with Miles and decided to go see Dame before I went. I hoped like fuck he was home because I so badly wanted to get this off my chest.

**

I pulled up to Damien's house around six. His car was parked outside next to a BMW in his driveway. For a second, I almost got upset at the thought of him having company, but how could I? I exhaled trying to calm my nerves. Right now, I needed Trinity more than ever. Her advice would set me straight. I've fucked up so bad and I needed to fix it. Tomorrow I made a mental note to go see my best friend.

I rubbed my belly as I picked up my phone to dial Damien's number. It rang about three times before the voicemail picked up. I hung up and pressed redial. Again, the voicemail picked up. I exhaled as I became irritated. I tossed my phone in the cup holder and grabbed my purse before getting out of the car. I marched up to his doorstep and rang the doorbell repeatedly. I waited with my hand rested on my hip.

The locks made noise as they were being unlocked one at a time. I tucked a piece of hair behind my ear as I became nervous all over again. Damien appeared in the door way and I was at a loss for words. He wore a scowl on his face. He wasn't happy about seeing me at all and that hurt a little. We stood there for a few seconds staring at each other. This was hella awkward.

He cleared his throat a little, "Wassup Jhalani?"

"Can I come in for a second? I wanted to talk to you." I said.

"Nah, I'm a little busy. What can I help you with?" he replied resting his forehead on his arm as he leaned against the door.

He was being cold on purpose. I wasn't use to that at all. I felt so pathetic standing there just staring at him. He just watched me through the screen door.

"I have something to tell you," I said looking at the ground.

"Aight? What is it?"

I exhaled, "I'm pregnant Damien."

He laughed a little, "What you telling me for ma? Aint you back with dude?"

My eyes stung with tears. I couldn't believe he had just said that to me. I knew I shouldn't have said anything. I should have just kept this shit to myself. He was being such a jackass. My feelings were beyond hurt. I thought we were better than this.

"No I'm not technically. I'm telling you because you're the father."

"I can't be too sure about that Jhalani. You gone have to prove that to me." he said.

"Are you kid-

"Baby, who are you talking to?"

I was cut off by another female voice. It completely threw me off when I saw Andrea hugging Damien from the back. I was stunned and so was he. He began stuttering.

"Dr-Drea, go your ass back to the room."

"You dirty ass, disloyal ass nigga!" I yelled as tears streamed down my face.

What the fuck was Andrea doing over here? She was running around here dragging Q's name through the mud and she was over here fucking his homeboy. More importantly, why the fuck was Damien fucking with her in the first place? It was some shady ass shit going on and right now I wished that Trinity wasn't mad at me.

"Jhalani! Chill man, it ain't even what you think," Damien pleaded.

"Fuck you nigga!" I yelled over my shoulder.

I walked so fast back to my car that I was damn near running. I cranked up the engine and sped away from Damien's house as fast as I could. By now, I was ugly crying. I mean straight up boo-hooing. I couldn't believe this shit! The audacity of this nigga to try and play me for a thot bitch. All that loyalty shit he spits and he's fucking his homie's girl. What a fuckin clown! Ugh! I was so mad that my hands were trembling.

I dialed Trinity's number and it went to her voicemail. I slammed my fist against the steering wheel. Fuck! Why wouldn't this bitch answer the phone? I needed to tell her what the fuck was going. Everything was just going so wrong and I was about to have a nervous breakdown. When I pulled up in front of my parent's house, Miles' car was parked out front. Could this day get any worse? He knew damn well he wasn't supposed to be here.

I jumped out of the car and walked up to his.

"Miles, you know you aren't supposed to be here."

"I'm sorry baby, I was worried when you weren't answering your phone. Are you ok?" he asked.

"No I'm not," I said honestly.

"Wanna go for a ride? We can talk about it." he said popping the locks.

I walked around to the passenger side and climbed in. I needed to talk to somebody to calm down. Miles was the best option right now. We were working on being friends so I should be able to vent to him right? He pulled from in front of my house and I relaxed into the seat. I was so overwhelmed and my body was tired. I didn't know where the hell Miles was driving to. It looked like we were headed downtown. I enjoyed the scenery for a little bit until I became too tired to keep my eyes open.

I felt a light tapping on my shoulder and stirred out of my sleep. It was dark outside and I couldn't see shit.

"Miles, where the hell we at?" I asked.

"My people's little rental property. I thought you might need some rest. Come on, get out."

I followed him inside the house. When we made it in, I saw that he had two carry out trays with him. He sat them on the small coffee table and turned on the light.

There was a brown couch and a small loveseat in the living room. Miles grabbed my hand and led me to the couch where we sat. He placed a tray of food in front of me and sat one in front of himself. My tray had baked chicken, macaroni, and sweet potatoes in it.

"This looks good. Where is this from?" I asked.

"Soul to Go." He replied. "You wanna talk about what was bothering you earlier?"

I exhaled, "Not really. I don't think you want to hear about that anyway."

"Come on, tell me. You were pissed so whatever it is has to be bothering you."

"I'm pregnant."

He stopped chewing and looked at me, "Seriously?"

I nodded as I stuffed a fork full of macaroni in my mouth.

"So that's what you were over there telling that nigga?"

I nodded again.

Wait! How the fuck does he know where the hell I was earlier? I stopped chewing and looked at him.

"How did you know where I was?" I asked.

He had this twisted look on his face and I instantly became scared. Had he been following me? He had to be. How else would he know where I had been?

"I followed you."

I closed my tray and stood up. I needed to get the fuck out of here.

"Sit down."

"I was about t-

He slammed his fist on the coffee table, "I said sit the fuck down!" he yelled.

I flinched and sat down. He pinched the bridge of his nose as he counted down from ten. This mothafucka was crazy. I watched as he sat there talking to himself, trying to calm down. I was scared as hell and didn't know what to do. This had to be a bad fucking dream that I was about to wake up from at any minute. I felt like I was back in my apartment all over again, this time with no escape and no one to call.

"Wh-why are you mad?" I asked lowly.

"Bitch, you gotta be fucking kidding me. I've been trying to do right by you. I go get a job, I clean myself up, get a little help and this is how you repay me?" he said through squinted eyes.

"Miles, I thought you had a girlfriend."

"That bitch wasn't my girlfriend. I had her pretend to be so that it would make you mad." He said looking at me from the corners of his eyes with a sinister smile on his face.

I felt like a complete fool. This nigga had been playing me all along.

"You cannot have that nigga's baby Jhalani. That doesn't fit into the story I have planned for us. You have to get rid of it." he said.

"Nigga what? Take me home Miles. I'm ready to go."

"If you think for one second I'm about to let you leave, you must be crazy," he said walking over to the door and locking it. He took the key out and stuffed it in his pocket.

Tears stung my eyes as I watched him walk back over to me and sit down. I was scared shitless right now. How the fuck could I have been so damn stupid? Really believing that he had changed. Now look at my dumb ass! Locked in a house with this deranged mothafucka and I have no clue where I am! I wanted to freak out but I had to remain calm. I didn't want to piss him off any more than he already was.

"So back to this baby. How are we going to get rid of it?" he asked putting his arms behind his head. When he did so, his shirt raised up and I saw the gun tucked in his waistband.

I felt defeated.

He looked down at the gun then back at me, "This is just in case you try anything stupid." he said. "Now back to this bastard baby you're carrying."

"Miles, I don't wanna kill my baby," I said with tears streaming down my face.

He roughly scratched his head, "Bitch you have to, so we can have a baby."

I became enraged. We had a fucking baby and he killed it! How dare he try and kill my baby again because he isn't the father. This nigga was crazy as hell.

I don't know what came over me but I felt like the Hulk. I jumped on Miles punching him repeatedly, landing blow after blow to his body. I was fighting for my life at this point. I needed to get that key or the gun at least to try and escape. Either one would suffice right now. We were tussling around the living room, knocking shit over trying to overpower one another. We fell and I landed on top of him. I dug my nails into his eyes as he struggled to pull me off. He kicked me in the stomach and I fell to the floor. This was happening all over again. I wrapped my arms around my stomach as I cried thinking about my baby.

I watched him struggle to stand and walk over to me. He stood there watching me cry and rub my stomach. He reached down and grabbed me by my hair and pulled me to my feet. I barely stood to my feet before he was dragging me to a door nearby. I panicked and try to fight again. This time, he pulled the gun from his waist and shot me in the leg!

BLAH!

The gun rang off loudly. I let out a gut wrenching scream and he snatched the door open and pushed me down a flight of stairs into a basement. My body was aching so bad all over, all I wanted to do was die. What did I do to deserve this shit?

I laid on the floor for a while fighting for the strength to get up. After a few minutes, I was finally able to sit on my butt and scoot into a corner. It was pitch black down here and I couldn't see a thing. I took my shirt off and tied it around my gunshot wound to stop the bleeding. I sat there shaking as I used my teeth to pull my shirt tighter.

I sat quietly in the corner with my arms wrapped around me. I kept hearing noises down here and it scared the fuck out of me. I didn't know what the hell was down here with me. It sounded like whimpering almost. Then I heard the sound of someone panicking like their mouth was taped.

I was getting weaker minute by minute. I was trying to find the strength to stand to find some type of light switch. After I was able to stand on one foot, I felt around for some type of string or something. After a few seconds, I found it. I pulled on it until the small basement illuminated.

I looked around until I spotted a girl tied to a chair in the corner. I drug my foot myself over to the other person and bent down to take the bag from over her head.

I gasped, "Sasha!?"

Sasha was beating up severely. Her hair was matted to her head with blood. She could barely see or talk through her two black eyes and busted lip. I cried again for her. She was in bad shape and barely breathing.

I lightly tapped her, "Sasha! Did Miles do this to you?"

She was so weak she could barely lift her head, "Y-y-es."

I heard heavy footsteps coming down the stairs. I turned to look up and saw Miles standing there watching us. He had this demonic look in his eyes that scared me to death. It was like he wasn't even there. He looked like a possessed person in one of those horror movies. Only thing is that this was real life and there was no director to yell cut.

"Miles, why did you do this to her? That's your sister."

"That bitch ain't none of my sister. Trying to get my mama to send me back to that fucking hospital with those crazy ass people. I was doing good so I stopped taking those meds. I didn't need that shit."

"What meds?" I asked.

"None of your fucking business. I don't need them."

I ignored him. "Miles, she needs an ambulance." I pleaded rubbing her hand. Her pulse was faint and she was barely holding on.

"That bitch just overreacting. Aint shit wrong with her."

I screamed, "Look you fucking maniac, your sister is about to die if you don't get her some help!"

His eyes went black and he cocked his head to the side, "What did you call me?"

The hairs on the back of my neck stood up, "N-nothing Miles. Please get your sister an ambulance, she's dying."

He shrugged, "Good. Then you can go with her." He pulled the gun from his waistband and pulled the trigger.

BLAH! BLAH! BLAH!

I fell to the ground, gripping my stomach. My insides burned from the hot lead that had just penetrated my body. It hurt so bad. I knew for sure that now my unborn was dead. I didn't mind though, at least this time I would get to go with them. My eyes opened and closed as I fought to stay awake. So this is what it felt like to die. I was at peace although I knew my family and friends would miss me. Being naïve got me in this predicament. I should have listened to that little voice in the back of my head. Now look at me, this is all my fault. I was so disappointed in myself for being so stupid.

Slowly the pain was subsiding and I felt ok. I took one last look at the ceiling above me and then it went completely black.

TRINITY

I woke up from my nap with a slight headache. Since my attack, I had been having headaches from my head being yanked back and forth. I looked over to my right and saw Q sleeping peacefully beside me. I was happy about that. My man had been searching high and low to find Geno's bitch ass. He hasn't been able to get any sleep worried about Geno still being alive. I remember the days when I prayed that nothing would happen to him and now I couldn't wait to hear the news of his death. Geno was real good at playing hide and seek. I just hoped he knew what he was in for when Q finally got a hold of him.

My phone had been dead for the last few hours so I plugged it up. I pulled the cover back and swung my feet to the floor. I made my way to the bathroom to grab an aspirin for this headache. I peed and washed my hands and then went into the drawer for the pills. I threw the pills to the back of my throat and cupped my hands to drink water from the faucet. I was too lazy to go downstairs.

When I climbed back in bed I had a text from Candice. I decided to check my social media accounts before reading her message. I had a few notifications from Jhalani as well. I had five missed calls and three text messages from her. I wonder what was so urgent. She had been hitting me up lately but it's been awkward as hell. After she told me she was still in love with Miles, I didn't hesitate to let her know how I felt. She was being plane fucking stupid for wanting to deal with that nigga again. Sure, I had contemplated on being with Geno again, but the nigga didn't nearly beat me to death or cause me to lose a baby. This recent attack was the first time he had ever put hands on me.

It was one thing to take back a cheating nigga but let's be clear, Miles was kicking her ass on a daily basis. For her to even consider giving him another chance was stupid as fuck. I felt bad after she left me at the restaurant that day. I had tried to apologize on numerous occasions but she wouldn't take my calls. I was hurt by that. We had been friends for far too long for her to shut me out like that. So lately when she had been hitting me up, I would just shoot her a text. It was all petty but I couldn't help the way she made me feel by shutting me out.

After I scrolled through my social media accounts, I checked my message from Candice first. She was asking had I heard from Jhalani, which reminded me to check her messages. I scrolled down to Jhalani's messages and read them.

BFF (6:07PM): *Sis, I'm about to tell Damien about my pregnancy.*
BFF (6:21PM): *Damien is a fuckin snake. I just left his house!*
BFF (6:22PM): *Let Q know his boy ain't shit! Damien is fucking Andrea!*

Did I just read that right? Did she say that Dame is fucking Andrea? I read the message at least three more times. I knew that bitch Andrea wasn't shit! Her fake ass pregnancy story about how my man wasn't shit, I knew it wasn't fucking true! What really shocked me was the part about Dame. How could he fuck Q's old bitch? I would have never believed Dame was a snake.

Q was about to be livid. I didn't want to wake him up but he needed to know this information. Shit was about to get even crazier around here. My baby and I can't catch a fucking break, one thing after the other. I exhaled and shoved Q a little. He snored lightly and rolled over wrapping his arm around me. I pushed him again.

"Q, get up," I whispered.

"Put yo mouth on it and I can," he said pulling me closer to him.

I laughed, "Ugh nasty, I'm not talking about that. For real baby, wake up."

"Shorty, a nigga dead ass tired. What the fuck you want?" he asked sitting up, looking at me through one eye.

"I got a te-

"Hold up, I gotta piss."

I rolled my eyes and watched him get up. His hard dick was standing straight up and it caught my attention. He noticed me looking at him and made it jump. I shook my head and told him to hurry up. While he was using the bathroom, I texted Jhalani back and asked her what happened. It was late so I assumed she would text me in the morning. I yawned as I texted Candice back to tell her what Jhalani texted me.

A few minutes later, Q climbed back into bed with a laid his head in my lap. I handed him my phone and told him to read the messages. He grabbed my phone and read the messages quietly for a few seconds. Q looked up at me with fire in his eyes. He completely sat up and reread the messages over and over.

He slammed his fist in the bed, "I knew that nigga was acting iffy. When did she send you that shit?"

"Around six. You okay bae?" I asked watching him rub his beard in deep thought.

"Yeah, shits smooth baby girl. It ain't shit. I don't give a fuck about him fucking the bitch. I don't care about her anymore, that's not the point. Where is the loyalty out to this bitch? Niggas just don't care about that shit anymore." He said shaking his head.

"Fuck em both. That bitch's baby probably belongs to him."

He looked at me, then shook his head, "You know what shorty? You probably right."

"That rat running around here lying on you knowing she wasn't shit. I can't believe yo boy though. That shit crazy."

He looked me in the eyes and said, "Baby, you can't trust a soul out here in these streets. Remember that."

He was right about that. I was stunned though! I couldn't fucking believe it. The way Q shows love to everybody, it's hard to see how somebody can snake him. Especially the nigga he came out the sandbox with. He looks out for Dame like I've never seen. For Dame to be on some fuck shit like that is crazy.

The more I thought about Dame, the more I thought about my best friend. I know she must be crushed. She had been fighting with herself to tell him about the pregnancy. When she finally does, she gets hit with a low blow like that. I was hurting for her. Although she had pissed me off, I still loved her the same. My sis was making a bad decision with the whole Miles thing but that wouldn't stop me from comforting her. Being pregnant was hard enough to deal with. Throw some stress and drama in there and you have a recipe for depression. I know she was going through it.

"Check on your friend T, make sure she straight," he said as he got up, "I need to make a few phone calls."

I laid down and scrolled through my missed calls. I found her name and pressed the call button. I knew she was probably sleeping but I was about to wake her ass up. We hadn't talked in a few days and I missed her like crazy. Her voicemail picked up, so I called again. When she didn't answer that time, I sat the phone down.

I pondered over what she could be going through. She would have had a baby already if it weren't for Miles causing her to miscarry. I know she badly wanted to have a baby by the way she acted when she lost the first one. I didn't give a shit what she was going through with Damien, I would make sure her child was straight the same way she does for Gio. I smiled thinking about the way she loves my baby. She treats him like she birthed him herself and he loves her the same. My best friend was going to be a great mother.

She needed to hear that, so I picked up my phone and dialed her again. The voicemail picked up again. I sighed and pressed the redial. I was going to call again and again until she picked up. Fuck it, she does it to me all the time.

After the fifth time, it stopped ringing but I didn't hear the voicemail. I looked at the screen and saw that time was going.

"Hello?"

Nothing.

"Hello? Jhalani? I know you sleep but wake up we need to talk." I said turning up the volume on my phone.

I heard breathing but still she said nothing. I hung up the phone and dialed her number again.

"Hello?"

I looked down at the screen to make sure I had dialed the right number.

"Hello?" they said angrily.

"Who is this?" I asked with an attitude.

"It's me, Miles."

I don't know why but fear and panic washed over me. Why the hell was he answering her phone? It didn't make sense. I silently prayed that she wasn't dumb enough to start hanging with this nigga.

"Why do you have Jhalani's phone?" I asked.

"She left it up here."

I rolled my eyes, I swear this dude was a fucking weirdo.

"Ok can you give it to her please?" I asked.

"No."

"What the fuck? Why not?"

"She's dead."

-To be continued-

CPSIA information can be obtained at www.ICGtesting.com
Printed in the USA
LVOW10s2109300816

502505LV00031B/1236/P

9 781536 910612